M000116854

CHASING
GOD
DURING
The Ever After

A Journey of Hope through a Costly Fairytale

VERA VICTORIA MCGRADY

©2020 All rights reserved. This book or any portion thereof may not be reproduced or used in any manner whatsoever without the express written permission of the publisher except for the use of brief quotations in a book review.

Print ISBN: 978-1-09832-695-1

eBook ISBN: 978-1-09832-696-8

This book is dedicated to my children, Isaiah and Victoria.
May you always seek God's wisdom and live a life of courage.

This book is also dedicated to those who cannot fathom
the impossible.
There is no peace like the peace God provides. He wants His
absolute best for you.
May you also seek God's wisdom and live a life of courage.

Chapters

Acknowledgments..1

Chapter 1: The Fairytale...3

Chapter 2: Single & Satisfied...7

Chapter 3: A New Beginning 13

Chapter 4: Bliss..23

Chapter 5: Uncertainty Continues but Perseverance Prevails.........29

Chapter 6: Facing Her Sad Reality..33

Chapter 7: Choices 39

Chapter 8: Blind Faith 43

Chapter 9: Anchored in Hope..49

Chapter 10: New Beginnings..53

Chapter 11: Divers Temptations 57

Chapter 12: Moments of Clarity 63

Chapter 13: Turning Point..67

Chapter 14: The Battle is the Lord's 73

Chapter 15: Passing Through Deep Waters...77

Chapter 16: No Regrets 83

Chapter 17: Waiting On the Lord..89

Chapter 18: Judgment Day..95

Chapter 19: Ask, Seek, Knock..99

Chapter 20: Moving Forward 105

Chapter 21: Steadfast and Unmoveable 109

Chapter 22: Joyful Thanks 113

Chapter 23: Trial By Fire...117

Chapter 24: Distractions of the Enemy..125

Chapter 25: Abounding in Hope and Peace..131

Chapter 26: A Brighter Day..135

Chapter 27: In Hot Pursuit of His Promises.......................................139

ACKNOWLEDGMENTS

Thank God for His amazing strength, His grace and His mercy. He is the keeper of my soul and the source of my every need. I give Him all glory and praise for His presence and His faithfulness.

I am grateful for some amazing women who shaped my character and had a major impact on my life. May they continue to rest in peace: Essie McGrady Callins (Mama), Otha Lee Davis (Granny), Mary B. Savage (Aunt May B), Joan E.S. Holden (Dear Friend), and Robin Fowler (Dear Friend). I have no words to describe how deep and wide the void that remains since you left this side of heaven.

I am so grateful for my children. I am overwhelmed that God would give me the tremendous assignment of raising them. My main mission in life is to give them back to God. Above all of the many lessons that consume my mind from day to day, I hope to inspire them to seek Christ first in all their ways. I want them to know Christ and to make Him known. I pray they will understand the fullness of God's love for them and the hope of His calling.

I am so thankful for Pastor Robert L. Campbell and his bride Minister Kathy Campbell. I am always inspired by their instruction, their example at church and outside of church, and their fruit. I am grateful for their love, support, and encouragement for my children and for me.

Praise God for Pastor Lewis Davis and Sister Carolyn Davis. Their prayers traveled for miles and miles to encourage me and strengthen me. They inspired this work within me six years ago. God's favor is truly upon God's Church and I am grateful for my union with them.

Praise God for the Kings and the Kings' Oasis - there is only one. It's the place where my children and I dream of being multiple times a year. It's not only a location but a presence that is full of acceptance. The love is both rich and pure. My children and I are spiritually refreshed in unexpected ways, and I have had so many moments of clarity. Our spiritual lives are forever evolving through this lifelong relationship.

I am so grateful for my dear sweet friends, who I consider family. We do life together regardless of the ups and downs. We support each other, we pray for each other, and we laugh together. No matter the season, our bond continues to grow stronger and I know they are examples of God's love for my children and me.

Thank you to Andrea Alicia Barilla, Freelance Editor and Writer, for providing an early manuscript critique and developmental suggestions to improve the structure and delivery of this work.

Thank you to Latisha Corpening for providing a second manuscript critique from a reader's perspective. Latisha is smart, wise and trustworthy. She is a woman of many talents. The breadth of her gifts is yet to be discovered.

Special thanks to Elder Teresa Huffman for providing a final manuscript review. I am so grateful for her prayers, encouragement, and spiritual covering. I am also very blessed that the Lord connected us so many years ago. Her friendship is true and unwavering. God knew this day would come long before we did.

I love my family and all those who played a major role in shaping my youth. I am blessed with a complex history but only by God's design. I am in pursuit of His purpose for my life. I am grateful to be a joint heir with Jesus Christ.

CHAPTER 1:

The Fairytale

"I will instruct you and teach you in the way you should go; I will guide you with My eye." Psalm 32:8

The day had finally arrived! Nina would finally be married to a man who would love and care for her. He was independent, mature and he was an entrepreneur. She believed they would build a great life together. It was the morning of their big day and Nina remembered an important errand she needed to run. She had received a notice from the United States Postal Services the day before that there was a package waiting for her at the post office. The interesting thing was that the origination address appeared to be their new home address. It was very strange but it sparked her curiosity. She knew she would not have time after the wedding due to the honeymoon. It was probably another wedding gift.

Nina drove to the post office with anticipation of all that the day would bring. After returning back to the car with the envelope, she quickly opened it. What she discovered would shape the course of the days ahead. What should she do with this information? What actions should she take because of it? It was her wedding day. Who had sent this information to her?

RED FLAG: Undisputable facts of illegal activities
Soon after parking at the home of a dear friend who was hosting her bridal breakfast, Nina quickly opened the certified mail containing multiple reports of her fiancé's traffic offenses – speeding, driving without a license, operating a vehicle without insurance. She tried to find comfort in the fact that some violations occurred almost twenty years ago. But as she studied the report a little closer, some violations occurred eight years ago, two years ago, two months ago, and last month. Then she read where he had been found guilty for *Common Law Forgery* just two months ago. She tried to process the

information but she couldn't. She placed the information back in the envelope and placed the envelope in the console of her car. She gathered herself together before going inside and greeting her closest friends on her big day.

The atmosphere was lovely, the smells of breakfast cooking were in the air, and the wedding party was prepared to share in Nina's big day. There was a lot of talk about the day finally arriving and what the next few hours would bring. Nina engaged in the conversation but all the time, her insides were strained with the information she'd read in the car. Obviously, it was very important for the sender to get this information to her before the wedding since they had obtained *A True Copy* of violations from two counties and they requested a return receipt for the certified mail delivery.

Nina tried to rationalize with herself that Charles had already told her that he didn't have a driver's license. What was he supposed to do? He needed to be independent and get to work. What else was he supposed to do? Not having a driver's license was inconvenient, but driving without a license was illegal.

Nina could not process the imminent fact of her reality. Instead, she allowed herself to drift away in the beauty of her wedding day. She convinced herself that her man had made some mistakes over the years but he deserved a second chance. None of us are perfect. He just needed the motivation and the love of a good wife to do the right thing. And, he professed to be a Christian. They would share a beautiful life together, and he would soon get his license back.

Charles had so much to offer Nina. After all, he owned his own painting business and his own home. Early during their getting-to-know-you phase, Charles informed Nina that he was planning to expand his current home and add two additional bedrooms, including a 24 X 24 master bedroom with a nice huge bathroom with whirlpool and walk-in closet. They would begin their life in a newly renovated home. Charles had lived in his house for approximately 15 years. The house was currently small and not much larger than a two-bedroom apartment. Charles estimated the renovations would not exceed $20,000. Nina knew very little about renovations but she was excited about his vision for them and his ability to lead. She would focus on the wedding and let him focus on the house.

AUTHOR'S REFLECTIONS

How could Nina have been so naïve? Why did she agree to date Charles, knowing that he didn't have a driver's license? Did she even consider how limiting and dysfunctional their lives would be with only one adult driver? Or, was she willing to accept the risk of him driving without a license? Maybe she wanted to show him mercy since his current situation was the result of past mistakes. Does a person's decision to accept Christ relieve them of consequences for past actions or decisions?

What about the long list of other misdemeanors, including forgery? Charles had not been forthcoming about any of these details and someone out there was certain this information would influence Nina's decision to move forward with the marriage. Unfortunately, Nina found out the morning of the wedding and she did not change her mind. She was too vested.

In Psalm 32:8, the Lord promises to instruct us and teach us in the way we should go. God also promises never to leave us or forsake us (Deuteronomy 31:6). He is faithful to do just that. Instead of asking God to direct her in light of each truth He revealed, Nina allowed her vision to be blurred by the possibility of a fairytale. Each time the Lord revealed the truth to her, she made an exception or an excuse. She allowed the flattery of Charles's words to cloud her judgment.

SELF REFLECTIONS

Have you committed to a relationship but you now realize it's a major mistake? Maybe you considered ending it but you're afraid due to possible shame, humiliation, or vested time. It is never too late to ask God for direction. Surrender your relationship to the Lord right now.

CHAPTER 2:

Single & Satisfied

"But you are a chosen generation, a royal priesthood, a holy nation, His own special people, that you may proclaim the praises of Him who called you out of darkness into His marvelous light." 1 Peter 2:9

Before this new relationship with Charles, Nina was quite satisfied as a young single woman. She was smart, fully engaged in her church, and she was a very thoughtful decision-maker. She sang in the choir, she taught children's church, and she was a leader of the singles ministry. Since she accepted Christ, she was striving very hard to live the way the Lord intended. Admittedly, she was not perfect but growing through every experience.

While she desired to be married, she had had enough heart-break to know that if it wasn't God-ordained, it would certainly fail. She was in a very good place but still seeking God's wisdom regarding relationships. How do you know when it's right? Is it realistic to think that a man would respect her celibacy in order to be in a relationship with her? These are questions she would ask. Some of her acquaintances thought she was naïve in this regard. She tried so hard to believe that if God said it in his Word, then that is how it had to be.

She prayed and attended bible study regularly as she continued to grow in God's Word. She learned to apply each new revelation. She didn't always pay her tithes, but once convicted, she activated her faith. This was also the same season when she was drowning in debt from school loans and credit cards. She was so diligent to get her finances in order that she got a second job. She was very conscientious about matters of home and matters of her heart.

Five years prior to dating Charles, Nina journaled:

I was re-born this weekend. I am at the infancy stage of "getting my soul back." Friday and Saturday I attended the Singles Conference in Greensboro. I learned so much about my life and the areas in which I need to grow. I have been saved for 3 ½ years now, but I have yet to learn how to live a pure and holy life. It wasn't until this conference that I realized that I can live a holy and righteous life, the way God intended, and still receive the mate that God purposed for me. What God has for me, it is for me. Since my last relationship, I've been so focused on getting involved with someone so that I could "get married." As Bishop T.D. Jakes put it yesterday, I have been idolizing "marriage" and "companionship."

God has me exactly where He wants me to be and I have been too ignorant to fully acknowledge His presence and His desire to be intimate with me. He will give me all of the love and company I need. I am alone but I don't have to be lonely. I have not been spending quiet time with God as I should. My ultimate desire is to be like Jesus. When I go against God's Word, I feel miserable and very uncomfortable! I can be pure and holy if I would just allow the Holy Spirit to occupy my heart and guide my actions.

As a woman of God, I should always respect myself and demand respect from others. This is the first criteria for establishing any relationship. The Lord loves me and He doesn't want anyone to mistreat me, especially when I am obedient to Him. Psalm 37:3 says, "Trust in the Lord and do good; dwell in the land and feed on His faithfulness." Furthermore, it says, "Delight yourself also in the Lord, And He shall give you the desires of your heart." Again, I've been placing my security in the wrong thing or person. What God has for me, it is for me. I don't even have to work hard or manipulate anyone to get it. When God determines that I'm ready to receive His blessings, He will hand them to me on a silver platter. God has created in me a woman who deserves great things, a woman capable of determining what is right and what is not, a woman whose ultimate desire is to please the Lord in everything I do. Why is it that I sometimes feel that I deserve less? Why do I forget that God is not limited to man's vision or capabilities? Just because a man is "together," independent and saved doesn't mean he is the man for me.

Dear Lord, my soul is so tired of these bad relationships. I am so tired of compromising my standards. I know that if I would trust You and serve You whole-heartedly, You will send my mate to me and he will adjust to my lifestyle and my relationship with you. Dear Lord, I want my life to be centered on you. You are the center of my joy. Thank you Lord for not turning me away but forgiving me for my sins!

AUTHOR'S REFLECTIONS

Nina was a woman after God's heart. Admittedly, she'd made bad choices and lost sight of her God-given value, but she confessed these insecurities to the Lord. She really wanted God's best for her life and she was willing to make the necessary sacrifices. At this point in her life, she was determined not to compromise her standards again. She would trust God to send her a mate who would also want to honor Jesus Christ as his Lord.

SELF REFLECTIONS

Are you often reminded of God's promises but continue to fall short in your decisions? I believe the Lord tests us with different relationships to measure our maturity and our faithfulness. It's easy to say what you believe, but how do you respond in faith when you're tested in your relationships? Do you compromise your standards (your Godly standards) for the sake of maintaining the relationship?

CHAPTER 3:

A New Beginning

"Unless the Lord builds the house, the builders labor in vain." Psalm 127:1

The wedding was everything Nina had hoped it would be – from the decorations and the music to the meal served at the reception. Many family members and friends traveled long distances to see this event. Apparently, Charles had a reputation for not committing, so it was the talk of the town! It was a beautiful wedding of two Christians who wished to honor Christ with their union. Nina was a beautiful bride.

Nina and Charles celebrated their union with a honeymoon to Montego Bay, Jamaica. They had a great time, but Charles seemed a bit preoccupied. Nina expected him to be all over her since they were celibate during their courtship. But it wasn't like that at all. They saw some sights and ate some great food. They even went snorkeling. It was nice and relaxing but lacked the excitement that she had anticipated.

Two months prior to the wedding, Charles began the initial renovations on the house. He got the construction permit and began the process. The real work began after the wedding. Nina had very little involvement as she didn't know anything about renovating a house and she'd never owned one. Nina and Charles stayed in Nina's apartment while the renovations were being made on the house. Then, one evening, soon after returning home from their honeymoon, Charles prepared Nina for a serious conversation. He said, "I have something to tell you. I would completely understand if you decided to walk out now. I missed a few payments for the mortgage because I didn't know where to send the payment. The address changed, and I didn't know who to call. Anyway, the house is about to go into foreclosure. I would completely understand if you wanted to leave me now."

Nina asked, "So is that why you were so preoccupied during our honeymoon?"

Charles replied, "Yes. I thought if we renovated the house and got it refinanced in your name, we could stop the foreclosure."

Nina asked, "So what can we do now?"

Charles stated, "Well, we need to get the majority of the renovations completed so that we can refinance it. We'll need to get a loan for some of the expenses, but we'll be able to pay it off when we refinance."

Nina was determined not to allow her fairytale to fall apart now. No matter what mistakes Charles had made in his past, she would have to forgive him. So much progress had already been made on the house – they couldn't stop now. Despite the discomfort in her gut, in the days to come, Nina would obtain thousands of dollars in loans (in her name alone) to ensure the completion of the renovations. Charles provided some funding from his business, but due to his poor credit standing, he could not obtain a low-interest loan.

Note to Self: A bad gut feeling is often the Lord trying to get your attention. Your gut feeling should not be ignored.

During the first six months of their marriage, Nina and Charles completed the renovations on their home. Charles added Nina's name to the deed, and the couple had the house refinanced in Nina's name only. It was during a time when appraisal values were exceedingly high in order to benefit the home owner. They were able to pay a large portion of their expenses as well as judgments that Charles had on his record. However, the new mortgage and remaining expenses were still quite overwhelming for Nina's salary. Nina had a good job at a local accounting firm. Charles had many expenses for his business, including payroll for his employees. He did not have a steady income for the household expenses. Nina decided that she would get a part-time job in order to pay off the extra debt they had acquired. She had worked as a pharmacy technician before in order to pay off debt associated with college, so she was not afraid of hard work and sacrifice.

After being married for only a short while, Nina got the biggest shock of her life! She discovered that Charles had stolen blank checks from an old statement, wrote himself a $10,000 check payable to his painting business, and forged her name – her maiden name. Her line of credit with her credit card company was the source of the funds he had received and used to give her money for the monthly house expenses. She was mortified! She cried and cried.

She called him immediately and he said, "I told you that I needed money to get my equipment out of the pawn shop and you didn't act like you cared." He ended the call abruptly as though Nina was at fault. What? Nina recalled a few months earlier that Charles seemed depressed and preoccupied. He eventually shared that he had pawned some expensive equipment to pay for their wedding and home renovation expenses. Nina had no idea. Charles explained that he had been given a deadline to purchase the equipment back and he didn't know what he was going to do. Nina tried to console him and told him to pray. Several days later, Charles seemed a lot better. He had also told Nina that he was expecting some money to come in soon and that he would have a paycheck for their monthly expenses.

Nina was beginning to realize that she was the source of the income he was expecting. Nina called the credit card company and told them that she did not authorize the payment. They told her that she would have to file a report of theft and credit card fraud and press charges against him in order for it to be removed from her account. She did not move forward with that option. She sat on her bathtub and cried. That is where she was when Charles got home. He had the nerve to argue with her about forging her name and obtaining money from her credit card without her authorization. He blamed her for not helping him with his problems. She finally admitted to herself and to him that their marriage was a big mistake!

Note to Self: When someone shows you who they really are, believe them.

Nina recalled when Charles first asked her out. Charles was a painter and Nina was a professional accountant. Charles had just finished painting her friend's house when he asked her out to dinner. Nina always wanted a professional man, so she quickly turned him down. More importantly, Nina wanted a Christian man. Following the advice of a close friend, Nina decided to pray about it before making a final decision. She certainly did not want to miss God's will for her life.

Nina mentioned Charles to a couple of other friends who knew him and each one brought up his past, which included several women. Nina just listened. She eventually came to the realization that he had never been disrespectful to her. She decided she would agree to them talking on the phone prior to any dates. She also did not want to condemn him because of his past. After all, we all have baggage and we all have made mistakes.

Charles told Nina that he wanted her to get to know him as a person and not just as the person who painted her friend's home. Admittedly, he had made a lot of mistakes, but Charles explained that he was immature then. He said that he wanted to be happy mentally, physically, and spiritually. Charles told Nina that he was a trustee at his church and he was very active. Nina asked Charles if he was saved. Charles told Nina that he was saved and that he was committed to understanding God. He said that he read his Bible every night but he did not understand it all. Nina told him that no one does.

Charles said that he had a good relationship with his pastor and that he often talked to him about things that he didn't understand. He told Nina that she could help him understand scriptures that he didn't understand. She told him that they could help each other. Charles also told Nina that he was not looking for a "girlfriend." He wanted someone who had the same desires out of life that he had.

At that point, Nina committed their relationship to God. Her eyes were WIDE open so that she wouldn't miss anything and wouldn't be naïve.

Nina's Prayer:

Father, I like the person that I see in Charles now. I especially like that he has a hunger for you. I don't know your purpose here, but it has totally caught me off guard! I commit my ideals, my desires, my emotions, and my physical desires to you and to your will. You are the Potter and I am the clay. Amen.

* * *

**Question: Are you in control of your emotions,
or are your emotions controlling you?**

Two weeks after Charles asked Nina out and a week of several phone conversations, Nina journaled:

I dare not write this down, but I do believe (and somewhat fear) that God has sent me my "mate." I get butterflies just thinking about it. I am so shocked and just filled with all kinds of feelings. I have known Charles for two years, and I hesitated when he asked me out to dinner. My heart is just pounding with excitement about this man that I've talked to for 5 days straight!

I asked him, today, why he all of a sudden asked me out. He said that he's been thinking about me for the last couple of months. He said that he thinks that I am the "perfect woman." He said that he knows no one is perfect and he's sure that I have flaws but for the most part, he thinks that I am perfect because I'm smart, intelligent, beautiful, together, and I have my head on right. I told him to please take me off of that pedestal.

We've learned so much about each other just within the last 5 days! And it's so amazing how much we have in common – we don't like beef, but cook it; we both like Catalina dressing (Ha!); we both are shy and get nervous when speaking in front of a group of people; we both like tennis (we'll have to see who has better game); we both prefer not to be in large crowds. How did he know that we'd have so much in common?

God really works in mysterious ways! He has allowed my spirit to connect to Charles's spirit first, even before the physical attraction (for me). Noel Jones said last night that the more two people have to compromise, then the less compatible they are! This is almost too deep for me! I'm just attracted to the voice on the phone, the person who I'm getting to know and it's so nice. It's like having a long distance relationship and spending more time on the phone than in person.

Charles told me that he's had his own business for 14 years and that he's just now beginning to reap the benefits from it. He's very stable, very mature, knows who he is and whose he is (God's property) and he knows what he wants! Is God awesome or what? God truly works in mysterious ways!!!

Note to Self: Be aware of smooth-talkers.

Later on the same day, Nina continued to journal…

Oh my gosh! Charles and I were just talking and he told me that he sees us building a future together! He said that he's very serious about us and that he is definitely not playing games! He said that he wants me in his future and he believes we want the same things out of life. He said that he will do whatever it takes to convince me, and that I am the perfect woman for him. He said that he prays that God will give us this opportunity, and if granted, he will move on it! He also added to a comment that he made earlier and said that he had been thinking about me for the last couple of months, and that he prayed about it. He said that he prays nightly that we'll be together.

RED FLAG – TOO FAST

I asked him if he wanted more children and he said that it depends on what his wife wants. He then asked me if I wanted children and I told him, "yes." He then said, "Yes." I asked him what he thinks his children will think and he said that they will love me once they get to know me! He told me about his plans to expand his house – it currently has 4 bedrooms but he turned one bedroom into two additional bedrooms, with a 24 x 24 master bedroom with a nice, huge bathroom with a whirlpool and walk-in closet in the bedroom. He asked if I would be interested in helping him decorate! He asked me if I was scared. I was honest with him and I told him that it was all so much to swallow and that it was all so unbelievable! He asked if he was scaring me off. I told him "no" and that I really can't describe how I'm feeling right now. He said that he will spend the rest of his life (from this day forward) making me happy! He said that he took a long break from relationships so that he could just think on what he wanted and needed. He kept saying that I am the perfect woman for him. He said that he is so happy that I am interested. He said that I have made his year! He said that he thought one time that he should have asked me out earlier so that we could have already been established (or seeing each other) but he said, "No, timing is everything." He said, "Good things come to those who wait!" I encouraged him to continue to pray about it. He agreed.

* * *

Three days later, Nina journaled:

I just talked to Charles and he is so confident that we'll get married. He asked me yesterday what type of wedding I wanted. My friend Lisa is still hung up on his past. I asked another friend about him tonight and she also recalled his past. I talked to Charles about it and he told me about the lady he dated for 18 years as well as a friend of Lisa's. He admitted that he has a messed-up past but he assured me that he is a different person today and he intends to prove this to his critics. I also asked him about his expectations during the dating phase. He said that he *has NO expectations other than for us to get to know each other. He told me that he is so confident because he has never prayed about a relationship before and that he is seeing God at work in so many areas of his life, including him having the opportunity to build a future with me, and he's NOT going to mess that up! He said that he's ready to fall in love with me and for me to fall in love with him. He said that for years his life was messed up because he didn't allow God to lead/direct his life. Now, he is able to win with God directing him versus before when he did what he wanted to do. He said that he prays every night that God would take control and lead him spiritually to do His will. He said that this is the last relationship that he will have. He said that he's ready for a few months to pass by so that we can plan our future together!*

Over the next several months, they met at the Christian bookstore for Bible study, they attended church together, and eventually they were in marriage counseling. People who knew Charles could not believe the changes they were seeing in him. People who knew Nina could not believe that she was marrying Charles. With the support of many family members and friends, they got married after a year of growing together.

AUTHOR'S REFLECTIONS

My pastor said that men are moved by what they see and women are moved by what they hear. Nina may have lacked this wisdom during her courtship with Charles. Charles was saying all of the right things, while remaining patient with Nina's standards to remain celibate until marriage. For her, these qualities were in perfect alignment with her vision for mate. Unfortunately, she allowed these qualities to overshadow the red flags that should have caused Nina to pause. She should have focused more on the evidence to support the words coming from Charles and not rely solely on the words. She should have heeded her gut feelings.

SELF REFLECTIONS

Think about you and your future mate. Do your personal criteria for your future mate encompass Godly character, such as integrity, honor, and honesty? Or, is there some misalignment between what he/she is saying versus what he/she is doing? How do you measure truth beyond words? How long does it take to obtain clarity regarding a person's true character traits? Have you observed actions that contradict your future mate's words? How will you respond?

CHAPTER 4:

Bliss

"Do not be yoked together with unbelievers. For what do righteousness and wickedness have in common? Or what fellowship can light have with darkness?"
2 Corinthians 6:14

It was a new year!

Nina continued to pray for the challenges between her and Charles. They were not equally yoked in their faith, finances, communications, or point of view. They did not share the same priorities. The adjustment to being married was very shocking to say the least. Nina had so many expectations of her new beau, but the biggest of all was that she expected him to be the spiritual leader of their home. She often became aggravated and frustrated because Charles did not spend dedicated time in the Word. How could he fulfill her spiritual needs if he wasn't fully committed to Christ? Nina continued to pray for Charles's walk with Christ, their finances – they had too much debt and insufficient income, and communication skills for both of them. It was one thing to disagree in everyday practical matters, but entirely another not to be able to communicate about them. She listened for details and asked a lot of questions. Charles did not like to be questioned and responded very defensively, deceptively, or totally evaded the question. Nina prayed that the Lord would calm her anger, bridle her tongue, and give her the appropriate tone to communicate with Charles so that he could receive her words. Charles thought he was right and Nina thought she was right. Nina even tried sharing God's truths about money with Charles but he had a higher regard for his street sense. More than anything, she wanted him to know that debt made her sick! He lived by a totally different motto than her. He often said, "It takes money to make money!" She understood there was some truth behind this statement. She'd heard millionaires speak of the risks they had taken and losses they had endured prior to their successes. However, their situation was totally different. They did not have a savings account and were living from paycheck to paycheck. She lacked security for their monthly expenses. How could they spend money they didn't even have? Nina needed peace. She was overwhelmed with the couple's debts and it was beginning to take a toll on her perspective of Charles and their marriage.

Nina journaled and prayed:

Heavenly Father,

I thank you for allowing me to see a new year! New beginnings always excite me! Just the thought of new possibilities, new opportunities and new memories is so energizing! I thank you, Father, that you've blessed Charles and me through the first 6 months of our marriage. Everyday hasn't been easy, but we are truly blessed that you are the head of our lives and that you continue to teach us and mature us through every test and every trial. Thank you, Father, for bringing us together! I'm excited about the many ways in which we'll grow together during this year alone.

My commitment during this year is to focus on the following by the leading of the Holy Spirit:

Strengthen my relationship with you by studying your word and spending prayer time with you.

Seeking your purpose for my life by completing 40 days of "The Purpose Driven Life" and applying your word to my life.

Spending more time focused on managing the finances for the business.

Spending sensibly and getting out of debt by setting specific financial goals!

Continue to eat wisely and exercise regularly.

Father, I pray that Charles will be filled with the knowledge of your will in all wisdom and spiritual understanding; that he may walk worthy of you, fully pleasing you, being fruitful in every good work and increasing in the knowledge of you.

Thank you, Father, for being so loving, so kind, and so faithful to me and to Charles, even when we don't get along or do not understand each other. Father, please give me wisdom to let go and just surrender these trials to you. I realize that I can't teach him and I can't change him. Increase in wisdom and knowledge can only come through you.

Teach me patience and long-suffering. Forgive me for making such stupid decisions regarding money. I will walk by your Word and your counsel. Please give me favor with my creditors right now. They are calling like crazy and I desperately need relief and favor.

Nina continued to pray and she decided to pursue a part-time job as a pharmacy technician. She hoped to gain some relief from all of the debt they had, but she also believed Charles was stressed from something that he had not disclosed to her. His solution to their financial problems was to apply for yet another loan. Nina agreed to apply for the loan to maintain peace in their marriage, even though the Holy Spirit was telling her that was not the way to go. Charles would not listen. He did not understand God's way when it came to finances and Nina let things get out of hand, as if she were learning this lesson for the first time! Thank you, Father, for denying us the loan that Charles wanted.

Nina prayed:

Father, please move within Charles's heart and mind in the following areas:

Give him a heart that wants to be just like you.

Give him a new language.

Give him a new mindset.

Give him your wisdom.

Nina thanked God for the job at the local pharmacy! Now, they would have extra money to repay all of the debt they had acquired. It was her desire to be a good steward of God's money. She promised not to ever mess up like that again!

Two weeks later, Charles's business was evicted. Nina prayed Phil 4:19, "My God shall supply all of my needs according to the riches of his glory in Christ Jesus!"

AUTHOR'S REFLECTIONS

Nina and Charles appeared to be at an impasse regarding their finances and they could not communicate. This is a deadly combination for a marriage! She sought clarification regarding money from God's Word and he valued knowledge gained from the world. She had to cling closely to the Lord during these challenging times for the sake of their marriage. Thank God He didn't allow their loan application to be approved this time! She was also willing to sacrifice her time to pick up a second job in order to pay off their debt! This was not how marriage was supposed to be. She endured more stress and aggravation since getting married than she did as a single woman. At the same time, she wondered that maybe working through these challenges was exactly what others had experienced in their marriages. She wasn't sure but she was willing to pray hard, pray often, and work towards a peaceful end.

SELF REFLECTIONS

Finances and communication are two of the main reasons marriages fail. I encourage tangible evidence of how a future mate handles money and finances. Make a date with your future mate to share each other's credit report. A person's credit report is very revealing of their character. It shows how responsible they are with managing money, how loyal they are to their creditors, and whether they keep their word regarding financial promises. On a practical note, it also shows existing debt that will impact you once you're married as well as their overall buying power for any future dreams you might have. Once all of your cards are on the table, how will you respond?

CHAPTER 5:

Uncertainty Continues but Perseverance Prevails

*"When you go through deep waters, I will be with you.
When you go through rivers of difficulty, you will not
drown. When you walk through the fire of oppression, you
will not be burned up; the flames will not consume you."*
Isaiah 43:2

Charles and Nina continued to follow two separate paths. He found a way to resurrect his business in his own strength, while she worked two jobs to overcome the debt they had accumulated. She was not enjoying this marriage that was supposed to bring her so much joy and delight. Instead, she was trying to maintain her integrity with creditors without going insane. Charles did not appear to care about the debt at all. Why would he? He already had bad credit. He was more concerned with his business and how others perceived him. She was angry with herself for missing this important revelation about Charles's character during their courtship. She was ashamed for disappointing God and she questioned how she missed Him while she was trying so hard to be intentional about her relationship with Charles.

At this point, they had been married for only one year when Nina prayed:

Heavenly Father,

You are so worthy to be praised, even in the midst of our financial burdens. Father, I am so tired of this debt! I set goals daily and I'm truly committed to paying off this debt. In fact, I am encouraged that I've just realized that the loans that we have with finance companies are 36-month loans!

"Have you ever seen a seed grow unless it was in dirt?" (Eddie Long)

Charles is going through so many changes with his business right now. There is so much doubt and uncertainty about tomorrow. Father, I am reminded that your Word says not to worry about tomorrow but sufficient for the day is its own problems. Thank you, Father, for your Word. Please continue to pour your wisdom into me! I need your guidance and your counsel DAILY. Please give me peace in my daily living; please give me more of you; please mold me during this time; prepare me for what lies ahead; strengthen my marriage and bless my husband! He needs you and your wisdom too!

AUTHOR'S REFLECTIONS

Nina was drowning in debt but she continued to chase God for His wisdom. She was past the point of frustration and what was worse, she suffered alone. Charles pursued his dream, regardless of the cost, discomfort or stress it added to their marriage. Nina blamed herself for the nightmare she was living but she continued to trust God more than ever during this season. She understood that "weeping may endure for a night, but joy cometh in the morning" (Psalm 30:5).

SELF REFLECTIONS

Sometimes we can become so consumed with shame because of mistakes we've made. In those moments of discovery, the best thing we can do is confess our shame to the Lord. Lamentations 3:22-23 reminds us, "Because of the Lord's great love we are not consumed, for His compassions never fail. They are new every morning; great is your faithfulness." What are you ashamed of? Today is a new day! Confess your sins today and move forward in His grace.

CHAPTER 6:

Facing Her Sad Reality

"The Lord is close to the brokenhearted and saves those who are crushed in spirit. The righteous person may have many troubles, but the Lord delivers him from them all."
Psalm 34:18-19

Nina often reflected on how deceitful Charles was regarding the house and how eager he was to renovate it. He already had sketches and plans when they married. He had grossly underestimated the cost of the renovations and he basically had nothing in the bank to pay for them. He'd driven her all around town to various finance companies to get loans to pay for the renovation expenses. And to top it off, he did not tell her the house was near foreclosure when they got married. She fought these thoughts for awhile but she was finally facing her reality.

After being married for only thirteen months, Nina prayed:

Father,

I know that you don't make mistakes, but I do. I wonder if I was supposed to marry this man. I wonder what is the purpose of our getting married? Was it for him to USE me to save his home, expand his home, pay for it? I wonder. I've been foolish so many times at this point of our relationship that I just wonder if I can survive it all. I wonder if my mental health will sustain this foolishness. How can a man who says he loves you drive you into debt to the point of you getting a second job, then buy what he wants to buy for his own pleasure? Was this my purpose? Am I supposed to feel this miserable and horrible on the inside? Am I supposed to feel this stressed and angry? Am I supposed to hate marriage this much? Was it also my purpose to experience DIVORCE? I have heard several ministers say not to ever allow the spirit of divorce to enter your marriage, but did I do this or did he? I cannot stand this kind of living. I did not work hard for all of those years to suffer and deprive myself like this to pay debt, debt and more debt! I hate living like this and I have never disliked someone as much as I dislike him. I would rather experience infidelity than this! Father, what do I do right now? Where can I go? I am dying on the inside and no one can hear me or help me but you!

* * *

The following day, she prayed:

Heavenly Father,

You have certainly reminded me of how to fall back into your loving arms! I love you so much but I am so hurt, disappointed and frustrated with my life right now. Your Word teaches me that you order my steps. Oh God. Your Word teaches me to trust in you with all of my heart, all of my mind, and all of my soul. I desire to be obedient to your Word – 100%. I want you to lead me in your way everlasting.

Yesterday, my flesh wanted to get out of this marriage! I was so unstable yesterday, so upset, and yet today, I'm reminded to "Be still and know that you are God." When I got home last night from my second job, I found a large 52-inch screen television in my living room!!!! With all of the debt and past due debt that is in my name, there was a big screen TV in my living room! Am I on another planet or what? Is he crazy? Exactly who did I marry?

When I got home tonight, I asked Charles if he would like to get counseling and he said, "I don't care. It's up to you, since you've already decided what you want to do anyway." Then I asked him who he would feel comfortable talking to and he responded that he didn't care, he doesn't need counseling. Anyway, he said it's up to me (in a very nasty tone). I told him if we're separating then we need to talk about that too. It seems our relationship continues to get worse rather than better.

On the following day, Nina prayed:

Thank you for a better day today, Father! I have tried so much to remember that my covenant is with you first, then with Charles. I have tried so much to remember that you're still watching over and protecting me and you're still shining and guiding the light that will get me through this darkness. I trust you, Lord, and I know that even though times are rough right now, you are still on the heavenly throne and you are more than able to turn any situation around. I know that you want only the best for me and for Charles. Teach me how to walk in your ways when he disappoints me and hurts me. Strengthen me so that I might be pleasing in your sight. I love you with all of my heart, mind and soul! Give me peace, Lord. Teach me how to exemplify peace even when I'm angry. I haven't forgotten the vision of peace that I had for my home. Help me to remember that I represent you at all times and to respond as you would respond.

I am so unwise and immature in your ways regarding marriage. When flesh rises up, I allow it to have its way. I know you're not pleased. Please forgive me, Lord, and help me to remember the testimonies of others who have suffered much worse or similar situations. This too shall pass. I cannot wait to testify of your greatness!

During the next few weeks, Nina became distracted because of an undetermined source of abdominal pain and bleeding. After going to the doctor for two weeks, she was finally diagnosed with a disease that had been dormant. She thanked God for keeping her sane. She felt defeated from every angle. Everything she worked so hard to achieve was crumbling right before her eyes. What was she supposed to do? How was she supposed to pray? How was she supposed to respond to her marriage? She had never been so distraught in her life – financially, physically, and emotionally. Satan was so busy.

She prayed: *Father, what are you trying to tell me? What do you want me to do?*

This was the first fourteen months of their marriage.

AUTHOR'S REFLECTIONS

Nina and Charles's marriage went from bad to worse. In the absence of any of signs of improvement, Nina began to entertain the possibility of divorce. She was working two jobs to pay their debts, while Charles was spending money they did not have. They could not be more opposite in their ideas about money. Yet, she remained steadfast in her prayers.

SELF REFLECTIONS

What are your personal views about money? Do you think Nina was overreacting in her position or do you think Charles had the right to spend money the way he wanted? What insight have you gained regarding this conflict between Nina and Charles?

CHAPTER 7:

Choices

"Therefore put on the full armor of God, so that when the day of evil comes, you may be able to stand your ground, and after you have done everything, to stand."
Ephesians 6:13

Charles and Nina continued to have their highs and lows over the next couple years – mainly due to their viewpoints regarding money and debt. Nina continued to work a second job until she had eliminated most of the credit card debt and convenience loans that were in her name. Two years later, Nina became pregnant and had someone new on which to focus. They were both excited to have a new life between them. Having a baby made Nina focus even more on minimizing extra debt and expenses. It did not appear to impact Charles in the same way. He continued to struggle with his business. Sometimes business was good and sometimes it was not. He even had employees who he'd have to pay each week and he would not bring home a paycheck. When income was good, he did not know how to carefully manage and store away funds for the less fruitful months. Instead, he enjoyed his television, his cable, and his suits. He wasn't willing to make any sacrifices so as to ensure there were provisions when business wasn't so good.

Nina had tried multiple ways of communicating with him when she did not agree with his choices. When they were newlyweds, she did not exercise any wisdom or restraint when she became aggravated. Over the years, she'd learned to try a softer approach. However, Charles would always tell her that that was "her way" of doing things and everybody did not have to do things "her way." He would also say that she just wanted to control him. She tried over and over again to "teach him" God's way but he would not listen to her. She also encouraged him to learn from others but his ego would not allow that.

One evening when Charles came home, he was driving a slightly used Audi SUV. Charles wanted to take her to dinner in the Audi SUV so they went to Olive Garden. He tried to talk to her about the vehicle but she was not interested. He had a jeep that he owned so she didn't understand why he would be interested in a vehicle with a car note. Having a child had now given her the confidence she needed to stand firm against any unnecessary debt and protect her name, regardless of what he thought. Charles kept the car for the weekend and mentioned that he needed her to co-sign for him since his credit score was so low. Nina did not engage. Then one evening the following week, he asked Nina if she was going to co-sign for him to get the vehicle. Nina told him, "No." He argued with her and tried to explain that he needed a car. Nina told him that he had a car. Experience had taught her not to assume any debt for Charles or anyone else in her name. She had already worked a second job to pay off debt prior to their baby. And, she knew her husband well enough at this point to know that he did not care about paying his bills on time, if at all. So where would that leave her and their child?

Charles continued to argue with her and became really angry. He said, "If you don't sign for me to get this car, we'll just be married in name only." Nina responded, "I can do you one better. We don't have to be married at all." He continued to fuss at her and use foul language. She called their pastor, explained what was going on, and gave the phone to Charles. She felt as though she had no other alternatives. He really expected her to give what she did not even have. She did not have money for a car note and neither did he. He always thought he had money that he did not have. He really could not see what he did not have until it was too late. If he wanted something, he was determined to get it without planning or making any sacrifices to get it. She was determined not to return to the situation she had previously experienced with him and all of the debt. He showed no signs or empathy for understanding how uncomfortable and stressed debt made her feel. There was a lot of tension in their house but she was so grateful that God gave her the strength she needed to stand firm and not be bullied this time.

Nina decided to separate from Charles when their son was 10 months old. She had had enough.

AUTHOR'S REFLECTIONS

Nina struggled to communicate her frustration with Charles's financial decisions. She wanted so badly for him to understand her point of view but felt he was adamant that he had a right to things that he had not earned or could not afford. It's easy to dismiss someone else's point of view when you are unrelated or when their point of view does not impact you. But what can you do when the opposite is true and the other person does not hear you?

SELF REFLECTIONS

Are you carrying a burden for another adult whose actions also impact you? Have you tried talking to them but have been unsuccessful? Do you feel ignored, helpless, and frustrated? Have you been praying for them? Ask God to give you the strength to stand on His Word and make choices that align with His Word. Leave the consequences to Him.

CHAPTER 8:

Blind Faith

"You never know how strong you are until being strong is the only choice you have." Bob Marley

How did she get here? She had so many high hopes and expectations for her marriage. She felt like she had given her marriage her all. In the beginning, she wanted to submit to her husband so badly that she somehow became confused as to what that means. God calls wives to submit to their husbands when their husbands are submitting to God. Nina had allowed herself to be abused and bullied by her husband. She never considered her situation to be abusive until a dear sweet friend described it that way. Nina did not know how she would manage the separation with her baby but trusted God to provide for her. And that is exactly what He did.

Charles stayed in the house, where the mortgage was in Nina's name. Nina and their son moved in with a friend initially and then an apartment. The rent at the apartment was nearly the same as the mortgage at the house, but it included all of the utilities. This now meant that Nina would have to pay rent and ensure the mortgage was paid as well. She trusted God.

Charles kept his end of the bargain and gave her the mortgage each month. He agreed to put the house on the market but he stalled. He really wanted to keep the house but his credit did not qualify him for a mortgage loan.

Charles visited their son every day. On special occasions, such as their son's birthday, Nina's birthday, their anniversary, or Charles's birthday, they would spend time together. Charles also agreed to go to counseling with Nina. They had several sessions with two Christian counselors who encouraged them to rehash each of their concerns. It was emotionally exhausting and mentally draining. Nina just needed someone to tell Charles how to add and subtract. After everything she had endured with him, he continued to blame her for his misfortune. There was no ownership regarding his actions and he lacked any humility.

Even so, after being separated for eight months, Nina prayed:

Father,

Please give me peace. I need more of you and your peace. I am so overburdened right now, but I am reminded of your promise not to ever put more on us than we can bear. I am so grateful for that promise but I need a breakthrough. Hear my cry, O Lord, attend to my prayers, please! Now that it is a new year, my feelings about Charles are changing. I am beginning to pray with expectations. I know that there is nothing that is too difficult for you!

Father, I just don't know what to do. I am so TIRED of this situation with the house. He still has not HEARD what I have been telling him. He is still working on getting the house in his name. He doesn't want to sell it. He wants to hold on to it… even though holding on means stressing me out and making me angry. I told him that I am not paying taxes and insurance for the house this year! He has had 9 months to get it together and there is still no progress. His mindset is still the same. I don't know, maybe I'm crazy for even reconsidering our relationship. He is selfish and so inconsiderate when it comes to what he wants. Maybe we are just so different in the area of money and maybe the safest thing for me to do is to pursue divorce. Even though it would be hard, I cannot change his mentality.

What if we reconcile and the situation gets worse? Then I could possibly have two children to care for and feel trapped and angry. Father, I need your divine intervention. Please give me peace and release —either release from the past, including the house, and/or release from the present, including the house! I want to be open to all that you have in store for me.

A few months later, Nina got a revelation. She wrote:

I feel the Lord moving in an awesome way in my life right now! I have been so overwhelmed by the trials regarding the house and Charles, but God spoke to me last week (May 4, 2009), "Are you going to believe what you see or are you going to believe what I've said?" How awesome is that! No matter what, I am to stand and trust God!

Place of Worship

While Nina was dealing with the challenges of her marriage, she was also praying for direction regarding her church. She visited a non-denominational church for three consecutive Sundays and knew she had to make another major decision in her life during this season of chaos. It felt like she belonged there. Every sermon was directed towards her and encouraged her in practical ways. Her faith was renewed.

The week after joining this new church, she received a call from her new pastor. He asked if she was married and she replied, "Kind of" but further explained that within weeks her divorce would be final. He asked for permission to contact her husband and he offered to counsel them. Nina consented and to her surprise, so did Charles. The two attempted counseling (for a third time) with Nina's new pastor.

Nina appreciated how direct her pastor was during the counseling sessions. He was wise, practical and knowledgeable about the Word and with regard to money matters. He knew how to talk to Charles about finances and convey how his decisions impacted Nina's trust in him. He also could see if Charles was genuine or not and Nina greatly appreciated this level of security.

As they received counseling, Nina continued to pray for God's direction in her life. She had always yearned for a husband and a family and now divorce appeared imminent. Her desire was to be in the Lord's will.

Happy Anniversary

Charles showered Nina with flowers, balloons, and dinner for their anniversary that year. It was also a month before they were scheduled for their divorce hearing. During dinner, Charles told Nina that they have a beautiful family and he loves her no matter what. He said that he had not given up on them. He also suggested they each get individual counseling before they reconciled. He admitted that he's been stubborn and he has always done what he needed to do to get by. Nina asked him if he could see how some of his actions were wrong and he said yes. He admitted that he had some problems. Charles also suggested that Nina receive counseling for everything that happened to her as child.

Nina admitted to herself that while she had been through a lot with Charles and they were a month away from their divorce hearing, she still wanted their marriage to work!

A dear friend shared a revelation that she had received and felt directed to share with Nina as well. This provided confirmation to Nina that God was up to something. She prayed:

Father,

I thank you for the confirmation that your hand is in this and that I did not make a mistake when I married Charles! For so long I wondered if I had misread you or missed your leading in the beginning. When I had my child, I knew it was not a mistake but I was devastated that my life had become a duplicate of every other woman who was once married.

On that same day, Charles said to Nina: "I don't know how you feel but I feel better about us now than I did 14 months ago. I think we owe it to ourselves, to the people who were in our wedding, and most importantly, to our child, to make this work!" Nina responded, "Okay."

AUTHOR'S REFLECTIONS

With all of the pain that Nina had experienced with Charles, she still wanted God's will for her life. It seemed that she was still holding on to her dreams of a strong marriage. She never thought she would be a divorcee or a single mom. The counseling sessions were painful and she couldn't really measure changes in Charles by what he said. Yet, she trusted the Lord to direct her path.

SELF REFLECTIONS

Have you found yourself facing a life-changing decision with the possibility of two very different paths? There can be so much uncertainty. God knows your heart and He knows your motives. You might as well be transparent with Him. Ask Him for the answers but also ask Him for the strength to accept His answers.

CHAPTER 9:

Anchored in Hope

"Many are the plans in a person's heart,
but it is the Lord's purpose that prevails."
Proverbs 19:21

On Sunday, July 5, 2009, T.D. Jakes said: "You cannot make a great decision if guided by your emotions. Stop asking yourself how you feel but what do you believe? Then, bring your feelings in alignment with what you believe. The land that I'm going to bring you into is nothing like the land you came from."

After a few counseling sessions with Nina's new pastor and gaining his insight and wisdom, Nina informed her attorney to cancel the divorce hearing. Charles and Nina reconciled, and Nina and their son returned home. Guess who paid the house insurance?

The remainder of that year was pretty good. Charles was very grateful to have his family back home. One day he told Nina that if they had sold the house, they probably would not have reconciled. Nina did not agree with the correlation but she didn't forget the comment. Nina paid the house insurance.

AUTHOR'S REFLECTIONS

Nina was not ready to give up on her marriage. She was hopeful that the counseling sessions and the near miss divorce helped Charles to hear her concerns and aggravation with his financial decisions. At least he admitted that some of his actions were wrong and that he had some problems. Nina wanted a normal life and she wanted her child to have a home with both of his parents.

SELF REFLECTIONS

Money and communication are among the top reasons why couples divorce. Do you applaud Nina and Charles's efforts to save their marriage with all of the challenges they had in these areas or do you think Nina should have moved forward with the divorce? Money can ruin anyone – regardless of whether they are married or not. Have you considered your own personal philosophy regarding money and whether it aligns with God's Word? Research scriptures about money and list them here. There are more than 2,000 versus on money. "For where your treasure is, there your heart will be also." Matthew 6:21

CHAPTER 10:

New Beginnings

"Therefore, if anyone is in Christ, he is a new creation; old things have passed away; behold, all things have become new." **2 Corinthians 5:17**

The following year, Nina decided it was time to discontinue birth control. Two months later, they conceived. Nina had Charles thinking that something was wrong with her when she invited him to meet her at her doctor's office. He was elated to learn that they were expecting. Needless to say, it was pure bliss once again. They finally had a happy home.

Nina knew she would have a girl. She had received a message spoken by Beth Moore that "God was redeeming the line." God knew that Nina could not handle having a girl initially because of the fear deep within which stemmed from her own experiences as a little girl. But now, the Lord was preparing her and reassuring her that He was restoring the generation. Nina acknowledged that God was at work through their seed and generations would be blessed and restored!

Nina was 6 months pregnant with their second child when she prayed:

Father God,

I am so consumed with our finances right now. I believe we have sufficient funds, but I've not made the best decisions. I need your guidance and your peace. I was so blessed in worship service today when my pastor's wife came over to me and whispered in my ear, "God wanted me to come over to you and give you a hug. He has not forgotten you. Heavenly Father, relieve her of her anxieties. Don't worry." Thank you, Jesus, for hearing my prayers. You love me and I have fallen short in my communion with you. I am totally committed to pleasing you! I have been coveting homes that I would prefer to have and I have not budgeted or managed the funds you've blessed us with. Help me, Father! Lead me to the right resources and change my mindset and my heart regarding Charles's carelessness with regard to life insurance, health insurance, and retirement. Lead me to do what is right and pleasing in your sight. What is my responsibility here? What do you desire that I do?

Over the next several months, Nina prayed for her husband and his spiritual growth. She prayed for direction regarding their son's school, and she prayed for the daughter they were expecting. She looked forward to explaining the story of how she came to be – after mommy and daddy almost divorced.

AUTHOR'S REFLECTIONS

Nina and Charles reconciled and conceived their second child. Was having a second child a driving force behind Nina's decision to return to Charles? In less than a year after returning home, she now has an opportunity to create the family she's always wanted. Yet, six months after becoming pregnant, she's praying about their finances again. Maybe it's just part of her DNA to think, plan and anticipate her family's needs. God sent a messenger in the form of her pastor's wife to let her know that He had not forgotten her.

SELF REFLECTIONS

God loves His children and He promises to hear our prayers. We have to trust Him with everything. We cannot pick and choose to trust Him in some areas but not in others. Have you put all of your cards on the table? He's our creator so He knows our heart and our motives. I encourage you to place your heart before Him and trust Him to reveal His plan to you. "Be anxious for nothing, but in everything by prayer and supplication, with thanksgiving, let your requests be made known to God." Philippians 4:6

CHAPTER 11:

Divers Temptations

*"Count it all joy when you fall into various trials,
knowing that the testing of your faith produces patience.
But let patience have its perfect work, that you may be
perfect and complete, lacking nothing."* James 1:2-4

D uring the year of their daughter's birth, Nina made only one journal entry. She asked God to lead her in her prayers and in her bible
study. She also asked God to teach her to be a better steward. Also
during this same year, God blessed her with a promotion. He was and still is
a good, good Father.

Their son was 5 years old and their daughter was 18 months old when
Nina prayed:

Heavenly Father,

*Please forgive me for the lack of diligence, focus, and perseverance in my
prayer life. I get so overwhelmed with everything that I need to pray about and it
has led me to worry instead. You've told us to be anxious for nothing, but through
prayer and perseverance we are to make our requests known to you. I am pleading
with you to move in these areas:*

*Let your will be done regarding Charles's business — one location or two.
The finances are draining us! He wants both but he is not equipped to manage
both. I want your will to be done! Please!*

Convict Charles's heart and give him understanding regarding your Word!

* * *

The following day, Nina prayed:

Father God,

*I am so overwhelmed with frustration and anger regarding our finances.
I feel like I carry most of the weight and Charles want to cut his payment short*

when it's convenient. Help me, Lord, because I am exhausted mentally. Thank you for reminding me today to "count it all joy when I fall into various trials, knowing that the testing of my faith produces patience." I am so grateful for your Word and I ask that you would please give me wisdom to handle this trial. Give me wisdom to manage our expenses smarter. Give me wisdom to explore other income opportunities. I am desperate and you are my only source of peace. Thank you for granting me peace and carrying this burden for me. I love you, Lord.

Sometime during this year, police officers came to the house to talk with Charles. When Nina asked about it, he said something about a customer giving him a bad check which caused his checks to bounce. His response did not make sense to Nina, so she just filed it (mentally).

As she became more overwhelmed with covering their expenses when Charles was unable to bring home a paycheck, she decided that they needed to change how they were managing their expenses. Charles was responsible for the utilities and cable and she was responsible for the mortgage, childcare, Internet, etc. One evening when Nina and their children arrived at home, their son was filthy and she was anxious to bathe him – but there was no water. She called Charles. He said he would take care of it. When he arrived home, he connected the well water to the house. According to him, the clerk downtown wouldn't accept his payment due to a delinquency with the water bill for his business. His explanation did not make sense to Nina, so she filed it (mentally). However, the water was brown and Nina was angry! She packed up overnight bags for her and the kids, and they went to a hotel. Charles came to the hotel later.

Nina was unclear as to how the water got fixed but returned home the following day. A month later, Nina was home with their daughter who had diarrhea and she was vomiting. Nina had given her a couple of baths that morning due to her soiled clothes. Charles called her and told her that he had been pulled over by the police and he was in jail. He provided a lot of details about how the police were profiling him and pulled him over. Then he reminded her of the situation with the bad checks. He said that he had to come up with $2000 in order to get out of jail. Nina just listened and he promised to keep her posted.

Nina continued to care for their daughter. After lunch time, she became hungry so Nina went to the kitchen to prepare something for her. There was no water. Nina stopped in her tracks and prayed for God's strength. Though she was extremely angry, she decided to call the water company herself. When she did, she explained her situation with a sick baby and she needed to get the water turned back on. The clerk was very nice and Nina appreciated that because she was so aggravated and embarrassed. The clerk confirmed that Nina lived at the address before she was able to discuss the bill with her. She said that the bill was past due for several months and payment of $400 plus was due. In order to accept Nina's payment, her name would have to be added to the account. Nina did not like this because she didn't want her name on bills that were in Charles's name. She could not trust that he would pay them and she did not want to mess up her good name and her good credit. But, she had to do what she had to do. She added her name to the water bill and paid $400 plus to restore their water. The clerk had said they'd be able to restore the water within the hour. Then, a few minutes later the clerk called back to say that the meter had been removed and that would cost an additional $200. Nina paid the additional money but couldn't get water until the next day. As it turned out, when she thought Charles had paid the water bill, he'd actually connected the well water to the house.

Meanwhile, Charles called to say that he collected most of the money he needed to get out of jail but still needed $600. He asked Nina for the money. Nina went off! She told him about her situation with their sick daughter and how she just had to pay to get the water turned back on so she didn't have money to get him out of jail. He was angry with her and hung up the phone! Nina thought, *"That's interesting. You're the one locked up."*

Two months following the water incident, when their children were almost 5 and 2 ½, Nina prayed:

Daddy,

I am hurting. What can I do? What should I do? I am so, so, so tired, angry, disappointed, and frustrated with the total disregard and lack of integrity in the man I've married. Friday will be 10 years! Wow! I am so grateful for my children but what a mess.

BUT, You are still Holy, Righteous, Mighty, Omnipotent, Omnipresent, Sovereign - You are my EVERYTHING. You will guide me into all truths. You still have a purpose and a plan for my life and I will trust in You. I will not be moved. I will not be shaken!

A few days later, Nina prayed:

Daddy,

Help me to see from your eyes and learn to think as You would have me to think. I am not afraid. I will not walk in fear. You have created me for such a time as this. Teach me how to lead with integrity and draw others to hear and receive my guidance – which comes from wisdom you've given. Open the eyes of my heart, Lord. I want to see You. I will bless Your name.

A lot happened in the next 6 months. Once Nina admitted to God what she feared to say for so long, she was ready to face yet a new reality. God prepared her for every step of the way. Nina received another promotion that summer. At some point, Charles bought another business by getting a loan from a private lender. It was a very costly and unwise transaction from Nina's perspective but he would not listen. Nina continued to pray and things were "quiet" for a few months. Then, they reached a turning point at Thanksgiving.

AUTHOR'S REFLECTIONS

During this season, Nina started to see more frequent glimpses of Charles's deception and lies. She did not want to face it initially, but it's hard to ignore an arrest or policemen showing up at your front door. She finally had to ask the Lord to show her what she was not willing to see. It was hard. She had the children she always wanted and they had an earthly father, which she did not have. These trials she faced since her return were a little different from the beginning of their marriage. She had to know what she was dealing with and face it head on.

SELF REFLECTIONS

God promises to shed light on darkness: "The light shines in the darkness, and the darkness has not overcome it." (John 1:5) When we're in relationship with Him, He tugs at our gut when something is off. He promises to give us wisdom when we ask and He is faithful to do just that. Are you in denial about anything right now? What is God trying to reveal to you? Do not be afraid. Ask Him to shed light on darkness. His strength is made perfect in our weakness.

CHAPTER 12:

Moments of Clarity

"Cast your burden on the Lord, and He shall sustain you; He shall never permit the righteous to be moved."
Psalm 55:22

Nina and Charles were barely hanging on. Her feelings for him and their marriage were steadily shifting south, although she was unsure what God would have her do. She felt that Charles sensed her distance from him. However, Thanksgiving had come and it was a season for thanksgiving. Nina was looking forward to a vacation away from all of her daily stressors. Some time apart might do them some good. As on previous trips, Charles drove Nina and the children to Texas to visit friends and family. Nina had planned to rent him a car so that he could return home for work then return to Texas the following week to drive them back home.

They'd made it to their destination and stopped to pick up the car Nina had rented. She left Charles there while she drove ahead. A few minutes after dropping Charles off, the car rental called Nina and said that Charles was not an "approved driver." When Nina questioned the reason why, she was told that Charles had an unpaid balance with their company and therefore he could not obtain a rental until and unless the balance was paid. Nina took a deep breath and thought "here we go, again." She told the sales representative to take the payment for his unpaid balance from her credit card that she had provided for the car rental that day.

When they both reached their friends' home, Charles did not say anything about what had happened at the car rental office. Nina was also suspicious about the phone calls that he had received during their travels. Once again, his responses did not make any sense based on what she'd overheard, but she filed it and did not pursue it further. Charles was very anxious to return home so after only about an hour, he got back on the road drove 12 hours back home.

Nina and the kids enjoyed their visit as always. It was always good to get away and have time to relax, reflect and pray. Charles returned the following week to drive them home. Once the children were asleep, Nina said, "You haven't said anything about the outstanding bill that I had to pay at the car rental." Charles replied, "There's a lot that I have to tell you." Something in his voice made Nina very nervous. Then he dropped the bomb. Charles told Nina that the IRS had seized his business and placed chains on the doors, all because of unpaid taxes from two years prior. At the time, the taxes were $26,000 and now, they amounted to $40,000 plus. Nina wanted to cry, scream, yell but she was silenced by her sleeping children and confined space. She prayed for the Lord to give her strength and keep her sane. She did not ever recall feeling this bitter about anyone in her life.

AUTHOR'S REFLECTIONS

Nina received moments of clarity in a matter of days. What she feared had become painfully obvious – Charles's noncompliance with the law, his mismanagement of money and his irresponsibility were causing Nina to feel as though she were drowning. She was bitter and angry. She had to cling to Jesus more than ever. When you marry someone, you're supposed to "become one." Yet, these characteristics did not represent who Nina was and she was exhausted from trying to correct Charles's mistakes or cover them up.

SELF REFLECTIONS

Do you need clarity regarding a relationship? Have you been in denial about something you are too afraid to face? Ask God to give you wisdom regarding the situation that is overwhelming you.

How do you handle moments of clarity that are not pleasant? Do you become emotional and erratic? Or, do you seek the Lord and bear your heart and soul? He created you so it is okay for you to take your anger and bitterness to Him. Nothing catches Him by surprise.

CHAPTER 13:

Turning Point

"All things work together for good to those who love God,
to those who are the called according to His purpose."
Romans 8:28

Nina and Charles made it through the Christmas holidays but all the while, Nina prayed for the Lord to give her direction. She desperately wanted to hear from the Lord and not step out of His will. She sought Godly counsel from several close friends but it was a dear sweet pastor's wife who explained that God does not expect us to be abused. Nina never considered what she was experiencing as abuse but it was. It wasn't a mistake here or there; it was repetitive, manipulative, unethical, and illegal behavior that threatened to ruin both of them and any chance of options for their children! Charles made choices like he was a 20-year-old child with no guidance. In his mind, he thought he was doing it for his family but he was ruining his family. He had a false sense of reality and he did not seek God's Word on any topics related to money. He did not realize that every choice he made impacted his wife nor did he seem to care. God had finally given her release from this marriage. She could finally admit to herself that what she ultimately felt was distrust for her husband. How could she continue in a marriage to a man whom she did not trust? She was tired of all of the surprise bills that he had not paid that always seemed to find her. He appeared to have no remorse or concern but rather a sense of entitlement.

* * *

Four months later, Nina prayed:

Dear Heavenly Father,

I am here. I am ready, willing and able. Have your way in my life right now. Direct my path and lead me to the resources to execute your plans.

In Jesus' name, Amen.

Over the next month, God led Nina to seek legal counsel regarding the appropriate steps regarding the children, initiation of the separation, and a new home. Nina remained calm as she moved from one step to the next. Charles appeared calm but lukewarm regarding the house. Initially, Nina stayed in an extended stay hotel but Charles did not like that and he volunteered to go to a hotel. While in a hotel, he searched for an apartment but he was denied due to a charge on his record. One night, he told Nina that she may have to co-sign for him. Nina thought, *"Really? Obviously, you don't realize why we're getting separated in the first place."*

After Charles stayed in a hotel for one month, he went back to the house due to the cost. By that time, Nina had secured a new home. God continued to show Himself faithful.

Nina's prayers covered her children and she diligently prayed for God's covering of her with regard to the marital home. The challenge was that both Nina and Charles were on the deed but only Nina's name was on the mortgage. This scenario set the tone for the next two years of battle that Nina had with Charles regarding the marital home.

She prayed:

God, I pray that you would remove my ownership from the marital home. I know I must walk out the steps of consulting with attorneys and taking action. I know that YOU will work this out for my good. You will not allow my credit to suffer or allow me to be put to shame because of it. Hallelujah!!! There has not failed one word of all your good promises!

Father, I pray you would guide me in regards to the marital home. I know you will protect me from the financial burden Charles has created for himself. Please show me favor with regard to that house. I count it done in the name of Jesus. Amen.

A friend posted the following encouragement on Facebook:

"Watch and listen, for I will reveal the areas of life where you have gotten stuck. And, I will give wisdom and direction with regard to your freedom. It is time for you to move on with bravery and boldness from the trauma and difficulties you have endured. As you let go of the past, it will let go of you, says the Lord.

Galatians 5:1: Stand fast therefore in the liberty by which Christ has made us free, and do not be entangled again with a yoke of bondage."

"Maintain your vital connection with Me, says the Lord, which will stabilize your life in these hectic times. Be strong, focused and unwavering, and it will help you deal with the chaos around you. You will also need to take time to quiet your soul and be still. Refuse to allow yourself to be drawn into things that steal your peace. *Psalm 46:10: Be still, and know that I am God; I will be exalted among the nations, I will be exalted in the earth!"*

AUTHOR'S REFLECTIONS

Through much prayer and confirmation, Nina reached a turning point in her marriage. God had provided the release that she needed. She was no longer confused about what it meant to submit to her husband. Submission is intended when your husband is submitted to the Lord. In Nina's case, Charles was abusing her financially and his actions had destroyed her trust in him. Charles did not involve her in his business decisions and he was dishonest regarding financial matters. When another person's risky behavior impacts you, you have to pray for release of that relationship. You cannot correct or control another adult.

SELF REFLECTIONS

Do you need release from a damaging relationship? Have you asked God for direction? Do it afraid. God is still God. He will protect you and cover you.

CHAPTER 14:

The Battle is the Lord's

*"Do not be afraid or discouraged because of this vast
army. For the battle is not yours, but God's."*
2 Chronicles 20:15

The marital home was the biggest battle Nina and Charles faced. This is the place where it all began. They say a man's home is his castle and Charles was so proud of their home. He enjoyed hosting family events and showing others the renovations. The original home, prior to renovations, belonged to Charles. He had convinced Nina that they should renovate it and refinance it in her name. After they were married, Nina learned that the house was going into foreclosure. Everything they had was riding on the completion of the renovations, a high appraisal value, and Nina's credit score. This physical house was a symbol for the spiritual foundation of their marriage. This house set the tone for the financial strain they would face in the years before them. This house was nice and spacious but just like their marriage, it was built on lies and it was spiritually empty. Charles was completely attached; Nina was not. For him, keeping the house meant stability and all he's known for many years. For her, giving it up meant release from the past and all of the ignorant mistakes she'd made. The challenge was that the deed for the house was in both of their names but the mortgage was in Nina's name only. This complicated matters even more. Nina and Charles had equal rights to the property but the responsibility for the mortgage ultimately lied with Nina, if she cared to protect her name and her credit score.

Nina met with a real estate attorney who provided specific wisdom regarding the marital home. He said the key is finding out who all has a lien on the house; then, once she had a buyer, the mortgage company would be paid first then they would notify other creditors that there's no equity in the home so that they can release their lien. Nina praised God in advance for protecting her and bringing her out without a spot or a blemish. She prayed:

"I am a warrior and I will fight in the manner in which you direct me! You have already promised that this battle is not mine but yours! I am the righteousness of God and I will stand tall from all of this! I am not defeated! Hallelujah! When it's all said and done, I will still be standing!

It was no surprise that Charles did not honor his word. He signed a separation agreement, stating that he would pay the mortgage while he lived in the house yet he only paid for a few months in the beginning. There was always an excuse for not having the money. Nina prayed:

Heavenly Father, please move speedily on my behalf! I trust you as I walk in your favor!! I see me the way that you see me and I will not be shaken! Though I stumble with words and actions, you know my heart, my qualifications, and my inheritance, and I will not be moved! Hallelujah!

How dare he think he can tie up or hold up my money (your money) while he lives for free? Ha! He doesn't even know. Father, fill me with the knowledge of your will in all wisdom and spiritual understanding.

Nina continued to seek the Lord's direction regarding the marital home. He told her to make the arrangements for the repairs, communicate the date/time to Charles, and follow through! She kept hearing God tell her to "follow through." Though emotionally draining, she did exactly what the Lord told her to do. Charles (in his ignorance) told her that he was trying to remain calm because he was very annoyed! The man who once was the smooth talker was now using a strong, threatening tone with her! He was living on her dime and yet he was annoyed! The nerve, the arrogance, the entitlement...it was not Nina's battle but the Lord's. No weapon formed against her would prosper.

AUTHOR'S REFLECTIONS

The actual divorce was a huge matter within itself but selling the marital home – the home Charles considered his – was an even greater battle. Selling the marital home would give Nina the closure and financial release she so desired but it would also mean that Charles would no longer live for free. When Nina considered all of the lies and ideas regarding the house, including the renovations and refinancing, she wondered if maybe marrying her was the last piece of the puzzle. The house was going into foreclosure and she didn't find out until after she married Charles. Deceit and duplicity do not pay.

SELF REFLECTIONS

What battle are you trying to fight? It can be overwhelming to fight a multitude all by yourself. God has promised to fight for us when we obey, trust and listen to Him. Nina was clinging to Him for dear life. She could only take baby steps as He instructed. No matter how angry, scared, or anxious you feel, give your battle to the Lord right now.

CHAPTER 15 :

Passing Through Deep Waters

"When you go through deep waters, I will be with you.
When you go through rivers of difficulty, you will not
drown." Isaiah 43:2(a)

The marital home was placed on the market October 1ˢᵗ and Nina declared it was sold. She did not anticipate what happened in the coming months. The next month she prayed:

Father, you continue to show me that,

I heard you correctly regarding this separation and the previous instructions regarding the house.

You are ever-present and You know what I need. You want your very best for me!

You are still in control! However, your timing is better than mine. You are faithful and you will not let me go down with this craziness!

Nina was aware of a couple of liens on the house that were in Charles's name, due to business taxes he failed to pay. After contacting the NC Department of Revenue and requesting a settlement for Charles's lien, they agreed to accept the greater of 50% of the equity or $5,000. Nina was so encouraged! This was way more than what she had even imagined! She thanked God for His favor in her life! She was overwhelmed by God's love for her.

While Nina was consumed with the legalities and financial matters regarding the marital home, Charles was struggling with his new reality. He tried opening up to Nina about his feelings for her. He would tell her that he missed his family and that he had not given up on them. Nina was not moved. As soon as she began to talk business with him regarding the house, his tone would change. That Christmas, Charles wrote the following note to Nina:

Nina,

I am writing you this letter because I need you to know something. You would think after 11 years of marriage that we could sit down and talk. I've asked on a couple of occasions if we could talk. So now I am writing, this is not a letter asking you to get back together. Even though I haven't given up on our marriage. I'm in no position to be the husband you deserve and need…financially, emotionally or spiritually. I need you to know that I take full responsibility for our marriage failing! I tried writing you this letter earlier. It really hurt when you didn't read it. At that time I wanted you to know that I was ready to do whatever it took to save my marriage. I was ready for counseling, ready to give up the business, etc. Because of my stubbornness when you didn't read the letter, I said forget it then. I allowed me being stubborn to ruin our marriage. There are a lot of things that I need to work on in my life to be a better husband and person. I had no example to learn how to be a husband, not making any excuses. I allowed the devil to come in our marriage and tear it up. We have a beautiful family, two beautiful children, that is a blessing that God has stored upon us, and I am so thankful. God has a purpose for our family. I intend to fulfill the purpose, for our family and for me. I have never wanted a divorce from you but I can't stop you from getting one if that's what you want. But I don't intend to give up on us. I didn't realize how I was away from God. The last year and a half has really humbled me. I have never wanted or intended for you to take care of me but you have been. That kills me inside but I intend to take care of that issue, I promise! My family is the best thing that has happened to me. I'm going to let God take control of our family in His own way.

Nina continued to move forward as God had instructed her with regard to the house. She was very familiar with Charles's emotional revelations. They did not reach this point overnight. No matter how much she disagreed with him and tried to offer advice, it was clear by his actions and total disregard of her position or feelings that he was someone who preferred to operate independently. From her perspective, he did not understand what it meant to have a wife nor did he understand how his actions, decisions, as well as inactions, impacted his wife and family. She recalled the police arriving to their house one Saturday morning and Charles telling her there were warrants for his arrest due to bad checks. He always had so many excuses and it was always something someone else had done. She was never quite sure of whether to believe his arguments. Usually, at some other point in time, she would learn there was additional information to a particular story or event that he had not shared with her. No, she had suffered for too long and separation was too expensive to turn back now.

Seven months after placing the house on the market, Nina received an offer on the house! The divorce complaint was served to Charles three days prior.

As it turned out, the offer was a low ball offer and quickly faded.

The next month, Nina prayed:

Heavenly Father,

You are my Almighty God and there is absolutely nothing that is too difficult for you! Please HELP ME! PLEASE! I don't know what to do. I continue to look at every expense that I have and I'm counting pennies to pay for gas. What can I do to manage fun activities for my children, buy clothes for them, repair my car, etc? What can I do? Help me, please. I think I am a good steward and I try to make good choices and live by your statutes. I am a cheerful giver, yet I am constrained in my giving. I know this is not the end of my story. I am waiting on you, Lord.

Isaiah 43:1-2

"Fear not, for I have redeemed you;
I have called you by your name,
You are Mine.
When you pass through the waters, I will be with you;
And through the rivers, they shall not overflow you.
When you walk through the fire, you shall not be burned,
Nor shall the flame scorch you."

I am considering foreclosure YET I know God has a better plan for me. It hurts so badly – I am truly exhausted – BUT, His plan is much better than my plan. I don't want an Ishmael, I want an Isaac. Give me peace, dear Lord. I know that you love me.

A Facebook friend posted this encouraging message a couple of days later:

Beloved, I would have you use your losses and setbacks to draw near to Me. Allow your faith to be perfected in the midst of difficult situations as you seek to know Me and My purposes more completely. Even in darkness, I am near, says the Lord. Remember that I am Your help and comfort in times of need. Psalms 119:50 This is my comfort in my affliction, for Your Word has given me life.

Days later, Nina continued to express her distress to the Lord. She did not know what to do. She was suffocating but she still delighted in the Lord. She trusted the Lord and she shared her heart with Him. She tried so hard to rest in Him.

AUTHOR'S REFLECTIONS

Nina is consumed with managing expenses for two homes — the one where she and the children lived and the one where Charles lived. Because of the evidence of God's promises as well as God's provisions, she was hopeful that the Lord would save her and answer her prayers. She continued to cling to God's Word. She had grown wise to Charles's tactics to win her back. He may have been sincere but he had not changed, as evident by his failure to pay the mortgage. He still did not understand what it meant to honor your word.

SELF REFLECTIONS

Do you feel as though you are passing through deep waters or do you feel as though you are drowning? God's Word gives us life! Do not succumb to the burdens that are upon you. Cast your burdens on the Lord and just breathe. God will lead you through the deepest waters if you keep your eyes on Him and trust Him. This is when your faith will grow bigger than your fear.

C H A P T E R   1 6 :

No Regrets

"Therefore I tell you, whatever you ask for in prayer,
believe that you have received it, and it will be yours."
Mark 11:24

After a year-long separation, Nina prayed:

Thank you, God, that my divorce finally became final. We would have celebrated our 12th anniversary this year. I am so blessed and grateful that God has carried me and protected me during that marriage. I feel like I have so much to teach other women who are contemplating marriage or who are in a bad marriage and don't know how to get through.

Father, I thank you that you did not condemn me or allow me to beat myself up for the things I accepted and/or allowed. You allowed us a second chance. Knowing all of the mistakes, I went into the marriage trying to love through the hurt and pain and betrayal. Now, I have no regrets. I am so grateful for my children. Help me to teach them your ways.

Now, though I was a mess two Sundays ago, after visiting the house and seeing the condition, I'm overcome with peace right now. Even though I'm down to $49 in my bank account, I still have peace because the end is drawing near! The drought and the famine are ending in my life and I look forward to sharing my trials with others.

I am so grateful for my Pastor. I met with him last Thursday and he challenged me to think beyond getting rid of the house because of everything I've been through to hold onto it. He suggested I keep it for investment property and consider it recoupment for everything I've put into the house.

I love you, Lord, and I know my latter will be greater!

Nina continued to move forward – even as she coordinated the children with Charles, while dealing with his arrogance and manipulation. She prayed for peace in the midst of the adversity. She searched for her new purpose in life as a single mom and single adult. She asked God to give her wisdom and to help her teach her children to be wise.

Two months after the divorce, Nina prayed:

I declare warfare over what belongs to me, in the Name of Jesus! I will go to court twenty days from now to resolve the marital property. I decree and declare:

Full ownership,

Charles's name will be removed from the deed,

Charles's full eviction in an expedient and peaceful manner, and

Rental property and an additional source of income for me, thank you Jesus!

Satan, you cannot have what rightly belongs to me.

Father, thank you for your strength that is made perfect in my weakness! No weapon that is formed against me shall prosper! Hallelujah! I declare complete health and safety over my children. Amen.

* * *

Nina's prayer continued:

Father God, I cast down every high thing that exalts itself above You! You are the Most High and You are Sovereign God! You are in control and You will reign!

Thank you for reigning on my behalf in my home with my children and outside my home in the battle for the house! You are TRULY AMAZING and I am overjoyed today because of Your love for me and Your plans for my life!

Nina continued to pray:

Thank you, Sovereign God, for reigning over all the earth! You are amazing, wonderful, mighty and above all! Everything You have created is beautiful! I am so grateful for the works of Your hands.

I understand, Lord, that You allow me to be tested and tried so that I will come forth as pure gold! Let me help others! I know and believe that you're allowing me to experience this fiery trial to:

Cleanse and purify my life,

Test me in the areas of my faith, endurance and devotion to you,

Demonstrate Your power to sustain me, and

Strengthen my testimony.

It is truly amazing to see how you've changed me and taught me through this whole experience! In the name of Jesus, I decree and declare that my case will be heard! There will NOT be a continuance and the judge will rule in my favor because of God's FAVOR over my life! I will have the victory in Jesus' name.

AUTHOR'S REFLECTIONS

Nina was experiencing the biggest fight of her life. She fought for her good name and good credit throughout the duration of her marriage and now following her divorce, she was still fighting for her good name and good credit. She did not receive release from God regarding the house. There were probably many days when it would have been easier to give up and let the house go into foreclosure but that was not who Nina was. To do so would have been a contradiction of her conscience and it would have discredited all that she fought for during her marriage.

SELF REFLECTIONS

God's ways are always perfect. All the promises of God are Yes and Amen (2 Corinthians 1:20). What is God instructing you to surrender to Him? Allow Him who began a good work in you to complete it (Philippians 1:6).

CHAPTER 17:

Waiting On the Lord

"But they that wait upon the Lord shall renew their strength; they shall mount up with wings as eagles; they shall run, and not be weary; and they shall walk, and not faint." Isaiah 40:31

The day of the hearing regarding the marital property had finally arrived. At 5:53 AM, Nina prayed:

I am beyond excited about today's events! I will have the victory day, in the name of Jesus! To God be all the glory!

I praise you in advance, Father, for going before me and setting Your victories in stone! You are in control of all things! You were there at the very beginning, and You are here today to give me the closure that I need! No weapon that is formed against me shall prosper! That includes any requests for a continuance! Ha! Ha! Ha!

All power belongs to God! I reverence you, God. I am yours and You are mine. Amen.

A couple of days later, Nina wrote:

God is STILL faithful! Monday's court appearance did not go as I had planned. After trying to negotiate with Charles for 3 hours, he decided he needed an attorney and requested a continuance.

During the negotiations, I told him that he needs to get out of the house. He said, "I can't do that. I would be homeless." What? You have commercial property and can't rent an apartment or a house? How crazy is that? I can't believe that he puts all of his energy into having a business and finding a space to rent but he doesn't use any to locate housing! Wow! It is ridiculous and crazy! But the main point is that IT'S NOT MY PROBLEM!!! Does he think he can pimp me to maintain housing for him? Absolutely NOT!

He kept stating that he wanted the court order to say he can re-finance. We are no longer married – it would be a purchase. Besides that, he must have forgotten that he has $40,000 in judgments!

I have many words to say about the entire situation but I will say GOD is STILL GOD and HE LOVES ME.

Psalm 37:7 ~ "Rest in the Lord, and wait patiently for Him; Do not fret because of him who prospers in his way; because of the man who brings wicked schemes to pass."

A few days later, Nina prayed:

I praise you, God. Where would I be if not for your grace? So many people are struggling with tremendous circumstances that I could be dealing with myself. You saw fit to remove me from one environment to another and provide Your favor upon my life. Thank you, Lord, for loving me so much and giving me new strength to deal with my own circumstances.

For some reason this morning, my mind was flooded with thoughts of how Charles has taken advantage of me regarding the house. I had it cleaned; I left really nice furniture, decorative items, etc. He has purchased a pool table and placed it in the living room. He's moved some things around that were in place for showings. He has rented a larger television and set it up in front of the television on the wall. He has placed the top half of the armoire in the closet. He has installed a shelf on the wall in the bedroom and placed a rented television on top of it. And, he connected well water to the house, which has stained the bathroom toilet, shower, and sinks.

Father, I know that You already know all of this! There is nothing that is done in the dark that is hidden from You. You have shielded me and carried me throughout all of this drama and I am so grateful for Your love for me! I am truly blessed and I will not give space for bitterness to take root within me.

I am reminded of Jeremy Camp's song, "He Know." I trust you, God. You are God alone and You are on Your throne.

I have committed my way to You and I am trusting You to bring it to pass! You already know the end of this story! And I know that You are the Great I AM! I have nothing to fear because You are my Shepherd, my King, my Father who loves me beyond words or people. I will continually walk in thankfulness and praise to God and feed on His faithfulness. Amen.

The battle between Nina and Charles continued to weigh on Nina but she was determined to rest in her Father's arms during this season. She prayed that:

Charles would be ordered to move out of the marital property and be ordered to pay back the mortgage that she had to pay since their divorce.

Charles's ownership would be dissolved from the deed.

She would gain full ownership of the marital property and full rights to handle the sale on the grounds that:

Charles had not honored their separation agreement. He owed Nina $21,000 in mortgage payments at this point!

He continued to make changes and modifications that decreased the value of the property.

Property was not showing at optimal level.

HVAC unit was no longer working and Charles had installed window units!

He installed a shelf on the bedroom wall for a television.

He connected well water to the house and it had stained the toilet, sinks, and shower.

The fish tank leaked so Charles moved it to the back deck and it was being damaged by the weather.

He placed a pool table in the living room.

Meanwhile, Nina continued to endure legal fees but God was so faithful to provide in this season.

Nina prayed:

Father, in the name of Jesus, I need Your relief! Please save me! This man has burned me more than once! He forged a check in my name for $10,000; he used my medical credit line without my permission to pay for $2,000 in dental work that I had to pay; and now, he owes me $21,000 in back mortgage payments.

Fret not thyself because of evil doers and those who prosper in his way. Evil doers shall be cut down like the grass and wither as the green herb.

Father, you've promised me that if I:

"Commit my way to You, and trust in You, You shall bring it to pass!" Hallelujah!

I claim it! I receive it! I believe it! You are bringing me out of this bondage!! I praise You and I thank you in advance!

AUTHOR'S REFLECTIONS

Thank God for Nina's relationship with Christ! Dealing with someone with such a skewed mindset regarding their own personal entitlement and grave lack of regard for its impact on others would drive any normal person crazy! Only Christ could keep her sane! She was determined to be obedient and patiently wait on the Lord. None of Charles's actions caught the Lord off guard. Nina could not control Charles's narcissistic behavior but God remained in control of all things. God just wanted Nina to draw closer to Him during this season.

SELF REFLECTIONS

Is someone mistreating you or taking advantage of you? Are you enabling someone's dependency on you? Ask God to give you revelation regarding your situation. Don't be consumed by your limitations or by what you can see through your limited vision. Rest in God's strength and let His power blossom within you.

CHAPTER 18:

Judgment Day

"The Lord is my light and my salvation – whom shall I fear? The Lord is the stronghold of my life – of whom shall I be afraid? When the wicked advance against me to devour me, it is my enemies and my foes who will stumble and fall. Though an army besiege me, my heart will not fear; though war break out against me, even then I will be confident." Psalm 27:1-3

Nina diligently prayed over the next six weeks, but even more important, she praised God for His presence in her life! She acknowledged his hand in multiple areas of her life. He met every single need and she was so grateful. She had a lot of credit card debt because she tried to manage the best way she could. When she really started to listen for the Lord's directions, she wanted to strengthen her stewardship even more. Besides purchasing clothes for her children and herself, she wanted to make her current home more comfortable with minor (yet costly) renovations, such as new carpet, new bathrooms, new kitchen. However, the Lord gave her peace and directed her to prioritize wants versus needs. She was managing two houses and there were so many unknowns with the marital home.

The day finally came when Nina and Charles's case was heard in court. After two continuances and so much wasted time over the course of several months, they would finally go before the judge. Nina was finally able to be open and honest about events that had happened regarding the house, how she's paying for her current home for her and the children, as well as the marital home where Charles was living and making things difficult for her. After Charles testified, the judge clearly knew he had a problem managing money. The judge explained that she was issuing an order that he pay the mortgage each month by the 15th each month. She also ordered a judgment for $22,000 that he owed Nina for back mortgage and he must cooperate with the sale.

Charles was very bitter for a couple of weeks but he knew the truth. Nina rested in the Lord's provision and His peace. She knew Charles would not be moved to comply with even these court orders.

A month after the hearing, Charles called Nina to talk. Nina just listened. Charles said:

"I was really angry. I really wanted to react and do anything stupid. The devil was doing something to me. I was so angry I didn't want to look you in the face. I didn't want my children to grow up without a mother. It took a lot of prayer and I'm glad I didn't react. You had every right in the world to divorce me. You had every right to divorce me. I had everything - beautiful wife, two beautiful kids – I had everything. I disrespected my family. I don't blame you. For years, I blamed you for a lot of things. I'm not telling you this to get in your good graces but because I needed to say it.

I feel like Job because I lost everything. It's humbled me a lot. It's taught me a lot. I was so far out there mentally. I was so far away from God spiritually. I was being selfish. I've been doing a lot of thinking, studying, trying to get a grasp on everything. I've been thinking I had everything every man would want. Pushed it away. I asked God to forgive me. I should have been a provider for my family instead of you providing for me. It's been rocky. I have no clue financially how to handle money. I made decisions on my own. It was never about me taking advantage or using you. We had a very rocky marriage. But the last few months, I've been humbled. This conversation is a reflection. I should have been that man to take that pain away. It really hurts. That wasn't my plan. There's a lot of other stuff I want to say. Please forgive me."

Nina replied, "I have."

Charles continued, "It was never a plan. God has a plan for me. I'm trying to find a job. The stuff with the house – it hurts. I'm trying to stay in His will. I'll be there in whatever capacity I can be for my family. We all mature at different times. I still haven't matured to where I need to be but I'm getting there. I just needed to say that to you."

The call ended.

AUTHOR'S REFLECTIONS

Nina and Charles's hearing was imminent for a while. Yet when it finally arrived, it was as though Charles was facing his reality for the very first time. Was he really that detached from reality or was it just his mode of operation to only deal with issues when he absolutely had to? And why did he feel he had the right to be angry with Nina? He didn't want her advice; he didn't agree with her approach; he thought she was trying to control him; he chose not to obey the law. He finally admitted that the divorce was his fault. At this point, Nina wanted Charles to comply with the judge's order. She was frustrated with the games Charles continued to play regarding the house but she did not have time to harbor bitterness nor did she have time for delayed confessions. She had to stay focused.

SELF REFLECTIONS

Has your back ever been up against a wall and you had no control over the circumstances or the outcome? Sometimes all you can do is profess the Lord's promises of His divine protection over your life. You can be confident that you will see the goodness of the Lord in the land of the living (Psalm 27:13).

CHAPTER 19:

Ask, Seek, Knock

"Now this is the confidence that we have in Him, that if
we ask anything according to His will, He hears us. And if
we know that He hears us, whatever we ask, we know that
we have the petitions that we have asked of Him."
1 John 5:14-15

Nina prayed:

> Dear Heavenly Father,
>
> Thank you so much for your amazing grace and your amazing power! I am reminded that you have given me the power to tread over scorpions and I thank you!
>
> Sometimes Lord, I want to do something extreme, such as stop paying the mortgage for the marital home or drop the price and take a hit on my retirement in order to sell it quickly! Every time I consider these thoughts, you remind me that these thoughts are not aligned with your plan for me. While I am frustrated, I have acquired patience and peace throughout this whole process. I have tried so hard to take my mind off of it altogether but I keep reading that I am to be persistent in my prayers.
>
> Father, I am asking, seeking, knocking – please relieve me of this financial burden quickly! If you have an amazing blessing prepared for me that involves this house, please grant me the peace to just hold fast to my faith as I wait on you! I am going to run and not grow weary; I will walk and not faint. I know you're working as I wait. I know that you're working things out for my good!
>
> I read Luke 18:1-8 where the widow persistently petitioned a judge who was not God-fearing nor did he have any regard for man. He gave her justice because of her persistence so won't you give me justice, Father, because of mine? I will continue to ask, seek, and knock!

I John 5:14-15 ~ "Now this is the confidence that we have in Him, that if we ask anything according to His will, He hears us. And if we know that He hears us, whatever we ask, we know that we have the petitions that we have asked of Him."

Hillary Scott's song, "Thy Will" became Nina's story. It reflected her struggle and eventually became her prayer because she no longer knew what to pray.

A month later, Nina prayed Psalm 31:1-5:

Father, You are a fortress in adversity!

In You, O Lord, I put my trust;

Let me never be ashamed;

Deliver me in Your righteousness.

Bow down Your ear to me,

Deliver me speedily;

Be my rock of refuge,

A fortress of defense to save me.

For You are my rock and my fortress;

Therefore, for Your name's sake,

Lead me and guide me.

Pull me out of the net which they have secretly laid for me,

For You are my strength.

Into Your hand I commit my spirit,

You have redeemed me, O Lord God of truth.

Father God, You hold my life, my future and even my present! Charles cannot do or try anything that You don't know about. You have promised to work everything out for my good! You have also promised that vengeance is Yours! I will not reclaim any bitterness. I am going to walk out every step, plan and instruction that You provide to me. You are my Master Creator and want only Your very best for me! Hallelujah! Troubles don't last always and I know You will rescue me speedily! Thank you Jesus for hearing my cry for deliverance! God, you are my Deliverer and I praise You! The devil will not gain a foothold in me! I will give no space for the devil in my life.

Thank you, thank you, thank you in advance for freedom and deliverance! You are my rock and my fortress! I have the victory in Jesus!

Thank you for wisdom, Father.

After she prayed, Nina remembered what her attorney had told her:

"You have a contract and the court can only enforce the contract. The court cannot determine new terms. The contract is to sell the house. Charles's non-compliance can lead to contempt of court and eviction."

AUTHOR'S REFLECTIONS

It was obvious that Nina trusted God to carry her through this process. She reinforced her faith through her prayers and by declaring God's Word over her situation. When we fill our hearts with prayer and praise, we leave little room for bitterness. God knows when we're broken-hearted and He encourages us to ask, seek, and knock. Even when we do not know how to pray, Jesus Christ will intercede for us. He will also guide us in our prayers.

SELF REFLECTIONS

It's up to you to ask, seek, and knock. God is waiting for your ask! He wants your dependency upon Him and not your own strength. Be as specific as you can be now, but continue to read God's Word so that He can provide clarity.

CHAPTER 20:

Moving Forward

"For My thoughts are not your thoughts, neither are your ways My ways," declares the Lord. As the heavens are higher than the earth, so are My ways higher than your ways and My thoughts than your thoughts."
Isaiah 55:8-9

Though the battle for her independence continued, Nina was hopeful and she continued to pray. There was no way to go but forward. It had been more than 3 months since the hearing when she prayed:

Father, I praise You for being my King, my Deliverer, my Master, my Friend, the Lover of my soul and so, so much more. You knew the very path of my life before I was ever born and Your view of my life is so much better and brighter from Your view. I will continue to trust You with everything I have. You work in mysterious ways and You make all things new. There is so much I don't understand and at times, fear has been my driving force. But, You have called me to be courageous! I am not worthy but You call me the righteousness of God! I am righteous through You! Why am I worried about money? You have brought me through amazing obstacles and You long to show me more of Your amazing works!

After much prayer, Nina reduced the price of the marital home and asked Charles to sign the realtor agency agreement.

He said, "I don't know why you're doing this. I told you I would pay you the mortgage."

Nina asked, "Do you have a loan yet?"

Charles replied, "I have to take care of a few things."

Nina stated, "I hope one day you will learn that you can't fix your credit when it's convenient for you. You've been working on it for 10 years."

Charles responded, "Nobody wants to buy the house anyway."

Nina stated, "Really? It's funny how your perspective has changed because when Tony was our agent, you wanted to sell the house for $300,000."

Charles stated, "You won't be able to sell it anyway until the liens are paid."

Nina replied, "Don't worry about that."

Charles added, "They can't talk to you without my approval. Who did you call?"

Nina informed Charles that she had contacted the IRS. The conversation drifted but Charles eventually signed the realtor agency agreement that noted a reduction in the selling price.

They had a showing on Wednesday and received an offer on Thursday! The initial offer was $190,000 plus $4500 in closing costs.

Nina countered with $195,000, plus $3,000 in closing costs.

The buyer countered with $194,000 plus $4,000 in closing costs and Nina accepted!

After the negotiations that evening, Nina attempted to call Charles but he did not answer his phone. She decided to give him space and let him work through his emotions.

Nina continued to pray for wisdom and she exercised self-control so that she did not contribute to any negative responses or actions by Charles. She also prayed that he would gain understanding about the right thing to do. He was so selfish! However, she needed him to cooperate and she continued to trust God to do miraculous things throughout the whole process.

Nina could also see how her confidence was growing in who she was. She was so grateful to God for that. He had so much He wanted to do through her and she was beginning to feel more empowered to be used however He saw fit.

At one time, Nina was so caught up in losing retirement money but now, she valued her peace and freedom so much more! God will fix and restore every bit and piece that is broken and she will depend on Him to do this for her!

Nina was determined to treat Charles with kindness, in the name of Jesus, Amen. Her focus was on God and His sovereignty! She believed in God's wisdom, His protection and His all-sufficiency!

AUTHOR'S REFLECTIONS

When you are experiencing victories during the lowest point in your life or while in the biggest fight of your life, it can be a big confidence booster! All throughout the pain, Nina watched the Lord develop her character, increase her humility, and mold her heart to reflect His desires. It was like David showing up to a sword fight with only a rock! God wants to show us how BIG He is! Sometimes we get in the way because we do not exercise gentleness and self-control. Casting your cares upon the Lord does not mean that you're choosing not to fight; it means that you recognize that the battle is spiritual and you're choosing to fight in the Spirit!

SELF REFLECTIONS

As women, we often struggle with when to bite our tongue. Nina was no different. There were lots of words that she could have released directly to Charles but it would have caused more harm than good. Ask God to help you identify when to talk less and pray more.

CHAPTER 21:

Steadfast and Unmoveable

"You will keep in perfect peace those whose minds are steadfast, because they trust in You." Isaiah 26:3

Nina had hope, again. She prayed:

> *My God, You are an awesome God! I am eternally grateful for your love, your mercy and favor upon my life! I trust You with everything I have and with every decision in my life. You continue to blow my mind!*
>
> *I have learned to let You be You! I will not worry about Charles's actions but I will trust You to move him to act when necessary. All glory belongs to You!*

Charles and Nina signed the offer. In anticipation of the payoff, Nina also completed an application for a loan from her retirement. She prayed for God's protection over her finances and she asked Him to limit the expenses of the repairs. Above all else, she prayed for wisdom and favor to fix what needed to be fixed and to negotiate the pay off of liens that were attached to the house.

During the initial inspection by the prospective buyer, the prospective buyer's real estate agent and the home inspector met at the house to inspect the property. Fully aware of the inspection, Charles went to the house during the inspection. The inspector found that the well water had been connected to the house and the City water was disconnected. The prospective buyer's real estate agent asked Charles about the connection of the well water to the house and told him that it was illegal. Charles argued with the prospective buyer's real estate agent which upset the prospective buyer. Consequently, the buyer terminated the contract.

Charles had sabotaged this potential sale. Nina maintained her peace of mind throughout all of this. She continued to pray and ask God for her next steps. Was she supposed to make repairs while Charles continued to live in the house or was she supposed to wait? What should she do? When should she do it? She was dealing with a selfish, unreasonable, angry and dishonest person who wanted nothing more than to live for free.

AUTHOR'S REFLECTIONS

Charles and Nina were divorced, and Charles maintained occupancy of the marital home while Nina paid the mortgage. Charles and Nina finally received an offer to purchase the house and Charles sabotaged the sell. Through natural eyes, it would appear that Charles was in the best position to manipulate any situation and control any potential sell regarding the marital home. But because of Nina's steadfast faith, she was not defeated. The Lord had allowed yet another opportunity to show Nina who was really in control.

SELF REFLECTIONS

Won't you let God be God in your situation? He has promised to never leave you nor forsake you and He is faithful! Rest in His peace and find His hand in your situation. Do not give the devil any credit for what you see through your natural eyes.

CHAPTER 22:

Joyful Thanks

"So do not worry, saying, 'What shall we eat?' or 'What shall we drink?' or 'What shall we wear?' For the pagans run after all these things, and your heavenly Father knows that you need them. But seek first His kingdom and His righteousness, and all these things will be given to you as well." Matthew 6:31-33

Nina prayed the words of Anthony Brown's song, "Worth."
Then she continued:
Thank you, Heavenly Father, for being my Master! It is because of You that I have an unspeakable JOY, even in the midst of being drained (for lack of a better word). I am so grateful that You paired me with Veronica Williams, my real estate agent, who has been nothing short of an angel! Veronica has moved forward, pressed and pushed even when I wondered "what," "how," "really?" Throughout all of this, You have made a way!!

Veronica contacted the City to discuss the status of services for the property and they would not discuss it with her without Charles's permission. Charles provided authorization for Nina to discuss water services with the City but he also said that he had no intentions of reconnecting the water.

Nina contacted the City about Charles's water bill and they informed her that the bill was:

$1,922.22 plus $165 for the meter replacement for a total of $2,087.22

NINA PAID CHARLES'S WATER BILL...AGAIN.

Nina finally had clarity – this was all about saving her name. She was "all in." Whatever the cost – if God provided (and He always does) – she resolved to pay whatever was necessary to dissolve her financial ties to Charles.

Nina prayed:

Father, You know my heart and You know my story. I will trust You until the day I die. Everything You've allowed to happen to me has purpose. I am available to You and for You. I will not walk in fear. It is You who has given me the power to produce wealth and I trust You with everything that I have.

Help me to be a good steward over what I have so that I practice strong discipline with my giving, my saving and taking care of my responsibilities. You are a God of restoration.

God will repay me for the years the locusts have eaten (Joel 2:25). If the powers of darkness have stripped and eaten the lives of believers, then God promises to make up those years and take away their shame. Hallelujah! Amen!

AUTHOR'S REFLECTIONS

It seemed appropriate that Nina would cling to the Lord's view of her as valuable. Outwardly, she was fighting for a house for which she was financially responsible, but inwardly, she was fighting for her integrity and credibility. She trusted her Redeemer to redeem the very qualities He had sown into her image. Nina finally determined that every resource she had came from God so there was no need for her to cry about using her limited resources in order to move forward as God had directed, because His resources are bountiful.

SELF REFLECTIONS

Though we are often overwhelmed with the lack of provisions from day to day, especially when going through a divorce or other unforeseen circumstances, or we feel like the devourer is consuming all of our resources, we must refocus and praise God for the mercy He has demonstrated in our lives. We must acknowledge that He is the source of our provisions and He will supply all of our needs.

CHAPTER 23:

Trial By Fire

*"When you walk through the fire of oppression,
you will not be burned up; the flames will not
consume you."* Isaiah 43:2(b)

Nina prayed:

Father, in the Name of Jesus, please HELP me! Rescue me from this financial burden and this situation that is consuming my life! I am desperate and I need You to act speedily!!! What can I do? Where can I go? What is the point of all of this? When will it all end?

On many days, Nina drove to work in tears because of what she faced with the house. As she prayed for the Lord's guidance, He made it perfectly clear that she was not to give up. Nina had to remember her recent moment of clarity – this was about saving her name and she had to continue to move forward.

Nina continued to pray:

Heavenly Father,

I thank You for being on the throne and being in control of my life! Please hear my cry and help me! I am in a place of despair and I am hurting. This man continues to use and abuse me.

What do you want me to do?

What is your plan for the marital property?

Should I take him back to court?

What will happen as a result?

If they evict him, will I get the full deed?

If they evict him and there is an offer, he will probably not cooperate with the sale. Then what?

What can I do in this secular world to either obtain full ownership and rent or sell this house at a price that I can live with?

Father, You have promised that I would not be put to shame. I am the righteousness of God. Greater is He that is in me than He that is in the world!! Give me wisdom, Dear Lord. I am more than a conqueror and I will walk out the path You have designed for me. Thank you, Jesus! No weapon that is formed against me shall prosper.

Nina continued to pray:

Thank you for being the Head of my life. Thank You, Jesus, for being my Lord and Savior. The peace that You give, no one can take away. You know my heart, my desires, my faults, and my imperfections. Yet, You promise to work all things out for my good. You said ALL THINGS and I trust You and Your Word.

You are busy working on Your very best for me even when I cannot see it. I trust You to be You and I will obey, trust, and reflect Your glory! I will not waste this storm! Hallelujah!

Nina did not expect the roller coaster ride she would experience over the next few days. She received the very best offer that she could have asked for – a young Christian couple offered $196,000 plus $5500 in closing costs! She was thrilled that these buyers were anxious to move forward! Nina was shocked by how smooth the entire process was, including the realtor's communications and negotiations with Charles. Nina anticipated pushback from Charles but he signed the contract and so did Nina. While Nina was basking in the excitement and hope that this drama was close to an end, the real estate attorney requested an urgent meeting with Nina and Veronica to share some new discoveries. The real estate attorney wanted Nina to make an informed decision regarding the sale of the property.

Nina was prepared for anything as she and Veronica waited for the real estate attorney to come into the conference room. Her faith was much stronger and she knew that God's plan would prevail. He finally arrived and told them that besides the $40,000 in the Department of Revenue and $1,000 with the Department of Labor, Charles had an additional $21,000 plus in judgments from personal claims.

More bad news. More evidence of Charles's real character. So many thoughts were going through her head but she did not lose hope. The real estate attorney explained that these situations are quite common. He wanted Nina to consider the value of spending all of this money for nothing but to save her name. The real estate attorney advised that since Nina had a house, a car and credit cards, she would be fine with the hit to her credit. He began to list out her estimated expenses (besides the liens and judgments) as though personal to him:

12% commission for the sale

Stamp and recording of deed

Taxes (prorated)

Closing costs

HVAC @ $5600

Water reconnection fee @ $2000

Inspection repairs - to be determined

Nina would have to bring $49,000 to the table in order to sell the marital home. (The Department of Revenue had agreed to accept a reduced fee to settle their lien.)

He said that he did not advise paying off the liens but told Nina to consider just allowing the house to go into foreclosure. In the worst case scenario, the default on the loan would go on her credit report but it would fall off in 7 years. Nina had been fighting for her credit for so long, letting it go was not an option!

After an in-depth discussion and understanding of how stressful, costly and time-consuming it would be to try to resolve the liens, Nina elected not to pursue resolution of the liens. Consequently, she could not honor the contractual agreement with the buyer. She could not sell the house. Nina shared with the real estate attorney that she would not let the house go but she would pursue full ownership of the deed and use the house for rental property. Nina's divorce attorney had informed her that due to Charles's contempt of court, the judge could now give Nina Power of Attorney to execute the sale of the property without Charles, or the judge could order that the deed be transferred to Nina. Since Nina could not sell the house due to all of Charles's liens that were attached, she would have to pursue the latter and use the house as rental property. The real estate attorney was very pleased with that choice.

The peace that Nina had after getting that news was a mystery. She wasn't anxious, angry or bitter. She felt more confident that God was making her path clearer. It was more obvious than ever that He did not want to release her from this house. Though it took a long time for her to realize it, she knew that the money she spent and sacrifices she made would not be wasted. God was still in control. Nina felt as though she was walking in a maze blindfolded, trying to figure a way out. But, God had bumpers and guard rails nearby that were leading her to see more and more of His direction! Wow! Within a few days, God showed her that even with the ultimate offer and circumstances, that He had something greater in store.

She was reminded of God's promise in 2 Corinthians 12:9, *"My grace is sufficient for you, for My strength is made perfect in weakness."* She was definitely at her weakest point. The only thing she knew how to do was move forward, while trusting God.

Nina prayed:

My heart was heavy after speaking with the real estate attorney but I continue to look to You, Father, as You are a Restorer of all things lost! You are intentional and I trust that You are STILL working things out for my good!

While Nina appreciated the attorney's thoughtful consideration regarding her situation, as well as his solid advice, she had not endured all of this pain and agony to just give up so quickly and take the hit to her credit! Over the next two months, Nina spent over $11,000 in repairs, $2,087 to reconnect the water, plus thousands in legal fees.

A week later, Nina journaled:

Sticks and stones may break my bones, but words will never hurt me. How many times did we say that as children?

She prayed:

Father, You are my refuge and shield. You are the Lifter of my head. Hallelujah! I praise You because You are my Master and You know everything about me, including how I feel and what motivates me to act. That is why it is so easy to love You. I don't have to defend who I am or how I think.

Charles is still the most ridiculous, selfish, thoughtless, and ignorant person I know. After everything that I've had to endure and correct in order to save my name, he had the nerve to say that I'm spending all of this money to get him out of the house in order to get revenge! Wow! He went on to say that he could have stayed there for four more months until he got a loan! Wow! He said I am hurting my children and after everything I went through in my childhood, I should not want to hurt them this way. He kept talking about when I asked for the divorce and how I didn't say why. He accused me of trying to "fix" him. Obviously, he has not worked through the craziness in his head. He continues to believe only what is in his head.

I pray that I don't let him into my head ever again. He is just a pure waste of my energy and I will not entertain the craziness! Thank you, God, for releasing me from that marriage!

Nina continued to depend on the Savior for her strength. That was the only way to remain calm and focused.

Two days later, she prayed:

Father,

Thank you for being my peace. In You, I am completely comforted. You are the Lifter of my head. You hold me and carry me through every situation or challenge that I face. Nothing that happens to me is a surprise to You. I will praise You in this storm!

My devotional today reminds me to "cease striving" (or "be still) and know that I am God" – Psalm 46:10.

Father, give me wisdom to cease from trying to explain why Charles is so wrong in his thinking. Also, give me wisdom to keep my mouth shut and not respond to his allegations about me. I cannot win with him and the conversation is pointless. You know all and You see all. My Charles Stanley devotional also states:

"My best response to disappointment is to trust in the Heavenly Father. Hardship not only forms our character but also reveals it. One common response to difficult times is anger. But instead of getting caught up in the emotion, we should wisely be still and trust in the One who can work everything for our good – Romans 8:28. I can only "cease striving" by trusting in Him."

Nina continued to pray:

So here I am, fully surrendered to You. What do You want me to do? What are my next steps? Who have You appointed to be my resources? You have commanded blessings to overtake me and I am about to explode!

Father, I do not want to be anxious or foolish. It is my heart's desire to fulfill your purpose and plan for my life. You have prepared me for such a time as this! I am fully equipped to handle this next phase of my life – filled with FAVOR, HOPE, PROSPERITY, and GROWTH! Enlarge my territory in the Name of Jesus!

You know better than me what my needs are and what I can handle. I am so very, very grateful and blessed that You wrap me in Your arms. You have not brought me this far to leave me.

AUTHOR'S REFLECTIONS

Just when Nina thought things were looking up, her excitement was short-lived and quickly shut down by more oppressive information regarding Charles. She had reached a new fork in the road. She could give up the financial battle, stop paying the mortgage loan, and allow the house to go into foreclosure, or she could assume responsibility for cost of repairs and reconnect the water in order to use the marital home for rental property, should the court grant her full ownership. At this point, Nina operated in full obedience to the Lord and she clearly heard Him tell her to move forward and trust Him. Others may not have understood her passion to preserve her integrity but it was who she was.

SELF REFLECTIONS

Have you ever faced a crossroad that challenged who you were or what you believed? Maybe those advising you encouraged you to take the easier, less strenuous path but something inside of you would not allow you to give up, even though the other option would require greater costs of you. Sometimes we have to open up our hands and give up even the very little that we are trying to hold onto in order for the Lord to perform His perfect work. He is the source of everything we have. If He requires us to give up even a little of our resources, we must trust that He is able to restore that little plus some. Obedience is better than sacrifice.

CHAPTER 24:

Distractions of the Enemy

"Beloved, do not think it strange concerning the fiery trial which is to try you, as though some strange thing happened to you; but rejoice to the extent that you partake of Christ's sufferings, that when His glory is revealed, you may also be glad with exceeding joy."
1 Peter 4:12-13

On the morning of Memorial Day, Nina prayed:

Heavenly Father,

Thank you for being an awesome God! Thank you for reminding me, through the story of Queen Esther, that you are always working out your plan for my life! Sometimes you're moving silently and softly and sometimes there are jarring disruptions! I have experienced both and I know that whether I can "see" the movement or not, You are at work on my behalf! I am truly grateful and I am so blessed that You want your very best for me and You have designed a purpose for me! Help me to fulfill it! Give me your vision and dream for my life! Hallelujah!

What would you have me do with this property? Should I rent it myself or use a rental management company? Should I seek a private renter or use as Section 8 housing? Lead me to Your divine purpose!

Nina was beating herself up for what she did later that day. Charles came over and begged her to loan him $1,000 until Friday so that he could close on the house he was trying to get. It was 2:30 PM and he said he needed to give his agent a check by 5 PM. He said, "I know you don't like stuff like this, but I am desperate. It was hard for me to ask you. My brothers will give it back to me to give to you by Friday. Nina asked many questions and she debated in her mind because she also needed to ask Charles to sign the deed over to her. That way, she would not have to go through the trouble and expense of going to court again. In her mind, she saw a very convenient way to put this saga to bed.

Nina said, "There is a situation with the house because of your liens."

Charles responded, "I was gonna sign my rights over to you."

Nina asked, "Really?"

Charles said, "Yes."

Nina said she would draw up a contract.

Nina spent the next hour researching contracts and typing up an appropriate one for the loan she was about to give to Charles. The whole time she could hear a voice in her head saying, "Don't make deals with the devil."

Nina gave the contract to Charles and he read it, then signed it. Nina gave him a check and he thanked her. One of the provisions in the contract was that Charles would voluntarily sign over the deed for the marital property to Nina the following day.

The next day, Nina contacted Charles about meeting to sign the deed over to her and he said that he was meeting with his agent all day for the house he was getting. He said he could sign it the next morning.

The next morning, Nina contacted Charles and he said he would get it notarized and give it to her. That afternoon, Charles said he gave it to his attorney.

Nina replied, "So you got your money and now you're not doing what you said you would do."

Charles replied, "I can't believe you went there." He said they could meet Thursday.

Nina contacted Charles on Thursday morning to execute the deed transfer and Charles agreed to meet. He wanted to just meet and talk. Nina explained the entire situation regarding the liens and Charles said his attorney told him not to sign it. He said, "I'm gonna sign it but not today. I will tell him about the judgments."

Wow! Nina had been hoodwinked AGAIN! With all of the craziness she had already endured with Charles, she allowed him to take advantage of her once again! She owned her mistake, repented for her actions, and resolved to stand on God's faithful Word.

"The wicked plots against the just, and gnashes at him with his teeth. The Lord laughs at him, for He sees that his day is coming." Psalm 37:12-13

On Friday, Charles returned $500 of the $1,000 loan to Nina but he never returned the remaining balance of the loan.

Nina thought, "Charles is a liar and a thief! He is deceptive and he's a con artist! The Lord will bring things around AGAIN so that Charles will need to ask Nina for another favor AGAIN! She will never trust Charles ever again!"

Nina's prayer:

I trust You, Heavenly Father, and I thank you for the compass of the Holy Spirit to lead me and guide me! If I don't receive peace from the Holy Spirit, I will not move!

Hallelujah! The devil is defeated!!! I will praise the Lord for being victorious in my life! He will keep in perfect peace, him whose mind is stayed on thee. I will not be shaken! The enemy will not get the victory today!

Holy Spirit, give me FAVOR with my attorneys and the court in this season! Thank You, Jesus!

AUTHOR'S REFLECTIONS

Nina has continued to pray throughout all of her trials with Charles. She knows that he is cunning, selfish and does not honor his word. Yet, when the opportunity presented itself, she thought she could trust him to sign over the deed to the marital home in exchange for a $1,000 loan. She was tired and just as desperate as he was. She thought she finally saw a way out of all of this. However, she ignored the voice in her head that reminded her not to make deals with the devil. She took matters in her own hands like Sarah did when she did not see God's promise manifest within her. It did not surprise her when Charles reneged. She had no one to blame but herself. But, she promised herself this would be the very last time.

SELF REFLECTIONS

Have you ever thought God was taking too long to manifest His promises to you? Did you try to fix your problem in your own strength? Were you satisfied with the outcome? God is waiting for you to submit your situation totally to Him. Don't try to maintain any of it. He is quite capable of managing it but He will not handle it until you take your hands completely off of it. Ask Him to show you where you lack submission.

CHAPTER 25:

Abounding in Hope and Peace

"Now may the God of hope fill you with all joy and peace in believing, that you may abound in hope by the power of the Holy Spirit." Romans 15:13

Nina often reflected and wondered why she was so behind where she desired to be financially, with all of the sacrifices she made over the years. She endured second jobs even though she had a professional career; she purchased used cars; she was a tither and giver. Yet, she had married a man who caused so much destruction and created so much havoc. Charles could not care less about his poor financial decisions, let alone how they impacted her or their family. She was always trying to clean up his mistakes when they impacted her.

After more than two years of stressing, crying, fighting, and enduring legal expenses regarding the marital property, God blessed Nina with the deed! It was not what she wanted or asked for in the beginning but God changed her desires to align with His. After hearing of Charles's contempt of court orders to pay current mortgage and back payments, as well as his failure to cooperate with the sale but instead, create new repair expenses, the judge ordered that the deed be transferred to Nina. Since Nina was getting the deed, there would no longer be an expectation for Charles to repay the back mortgage or the repair expenses, which he had no intentions of paying anyway.

Nina actually witnessed her Lord and Savior "bringing forth her justice as the noonday."

* * *

Nina's prayer:

Heavenly Father – Abba Father,

Thank you, thank you, thank you!! You blew my mind today! After more than two years of fighting Charles for the marital property, You have blessed me to get the deed! Hallelujah! You are amazing!

God, You are amazing! I will bless the Lord at all times! His praise shall continually be in my mouth! You have shown me Your truths while I trusted You! You still loved me enough to show me! Your Word continues to be true! I know that You want your absolute best for me!

Nina obtained guidance regarding the rental agreements, advertisements, etc. Within three hours of posting the listing, she had received three phone calls from potential renters. The first caller called again three days later and did not want to wait until after the cleaning to see the property. These callers became Nina's first renters.

Nina continued to trust God as she moved through this new phase. Even though Charles had moved out of the marital property, Nina knew he was angry. Charles had left some large items at the house that needed to be removed. Nina sent him a text and requested that the items be removed by the end of the following day. Charles threatened her when she saw him later that day. He said, "Don't push me. That is why men do what they do. Don't push me. I've been nice this whole time because of my kids."

* * *

Nina's prayer:

I decree and declare that God has not given me a spirit of fear, but of power, love, and a sound mind! Hallelujah! Whatever harm he plans or wishes upon me, has already been done to him in the name of Jesus! I do not walk alone and I am not afraid!

I declare PEACE! "He will keep him in perfect PEACE whose mind is stayed on You, because he trusts in You." – Isaiah 26:3

AUTHOR'S REFLECTIONS

Divorce and the resolution of property and material posses-
sions can bring out the worst in people. With all that Nina did
to pay for expenses during their marriage, pay the mortgage
after their divorce, plus extend a loan that was not repaid,
Charles was still angry and blamed her for his choices. She did
not even want the house. Had he been loyal to his creditors,
he could have secured a loan for the house and Nina would
have been happy with that. It certainly would have saved her
legal expenses, house repairs, time and aggravation. Instead,
Charles felt entitled and accepted no responsibility for his
choices or his actions. God honored Nina's faithfulness and
obedience.

SELF REFLECTIONS

If you're feeling exhausted from the weight of dissolving a marriage or a relationship, God wants you to cast your cares on
Him. Study His Word and ask Him to give you peace and direction. You cannot walk in fear. Let your faith be bigger than your
fear. God will blow your mind. Admit your fears to Him and ask
Him to give you understanding through His Word.

CHAPTER 26:

A Brighter Day

"The Lord is not slow in keeping His promise, as some understand slowness. Instead He is patient with you, not wanting anyone to perish, but everyone to come to repentance." 2 Peter 3:9

Nina continued to praise God for the battle He had won. She was not responsible for Charles's actions or words but only her own. She was focused on managing her children, her work, her residence and the rental property.

Three months later, Charles called her at work and said the following:

"I was really angry. I really wanted to react and do something stupid. The devil was doing that to me. I was so angry, I didn't want to look you in the face. I didn't want my children to grow up without a mother. It took a lot of prayer and I'm glad I didn't react.

You had every right in the world to divorce me. I had everything – a beautiful wife, two beautiful kids – I had everything. I disrespected my family. I don't blame you. For years, I blamed you for a lot of things. I'm not telling you to get in your good graces but because I needed to say it.

I feel like Job because I lost everything. It's humbled me a lot. It's taught me a lot. I was so far out there mentally. I was so far away from God, spiritually. I was being selfish. I've been doing a lot of thinking and studying and trying to get a grasp on everything. I've been thinking I had everything any man would want. I pushed it away. I asked God to forgive me. I should have been a provider for my family instead of you providing for me. I have no clue financially how to handle money. I made decisions on my own. It was never about me taking advantage or using you. We had a very rocky marriage.

The last few months, I have been humbled. This conversation is a reflection. I should have been that man to take that pain away. It really hurts. That wasn't my plan. There is a lot of other stuff that I want to say. Please forgive me. It was never a plan.

God has a plan for me. I'm trying to find a job. The stuff with the house really hurt. I'm trying to stay in his will. I want to be there in whatever capacity I can be for my family. We all mature at different times. I still haven't matured to where I need to be but I'm getting there. I just needed to say that to you."

AUTHOR'S REFLECTIONS

Though Nina believed Charles's comments were heartfelt, they were not new to her. There had been other occasions when Charles would get a revelation and he would apologize. Just like in this instance, his apology was much too late and after much heartbreak. When does a person start thinking before they act and do what is right so there is no need for apologizing over and over? Nina just listened. It was the best way to maintain peace. It may have given him some relief to share from his heart but it didn't change anything from her perspective. None of her words she'd spoken during their marriage or the divorce had made a difference so there was nothing she could say at this point. She had already forgiven him for her own peace of mind.

SELF REFLECTIONS

Have you ever received a heartfelt apology after a lot of pain and negative experiences? Were you confused about how to react to the apology? Some people think forgiving a person means to go back to a relationship or allow someone back into your life. That is not the case. Forgiveness means that you will try very hard not to allow bitterness to consume you when you think of that person, talk to that person, or deal with that person. Forgiveness means that you will allow Christ to rule in and through your heart so that it's Him that others see and not your ugly flesh. Are you harboring anger or bitterness towards someone right now? Give it to God so that it no longer damages your soul.

CHAPTER 27:

In Hot Pursuit of His Promises

"For I know the thoughts that I think toward you, says the Lord, thoughts of peace and not of evil, to give you a future and a hope. Then you will call upon Me and go and pray to Me, and I will listen to you. And you will seek Me and find Me when you search for Me with all your heart." Jeremiah 29:11-13

Nina had some reflections of her own.

Sometimes we do not see who a person really is because we are busy trying to see who we want them to be. She recalled a sermon by Rev. Jonathan Shaw who said, "Sometimes God shows you what you don't want before he shows you the right one." Nina still believed there was purpose in her marriage to Charles but there were several red flags that she believes should have redirected her.

She also recalled a minister stating "if it's not practical, it's not spiritual." Due to bad choices as a young adult and multiple incidents since that time, Charles did not even have a driver's license when they discussed marriage. Somehow Nina thought she could help him be better but she later realized that it wasn't her job to fix him. He had to be accountable to Christ and it wasn't her job to be his savior in any way – not spiritually or financially.

Charles's credit report told a lot about who he was and where he was but Nina did not even ask to see it prior to marriage. Looking at a potential spouse's credit report is not the first thing you think about when discussing marriage but had they reviewed each other's reports, Nina would have learned of Charles's lack of loyalty to his creditors. A person's commitment to honor their loan agreements reflects their level of maturity, ownership and responsibility. It is true that things happen sometimes outside of our control but those challenges must drive future actions and choices. If you didn't honor your last creditor, why should a new creditor trust you? This is the practical side of being equally yoked with your mate. Paying off her debt and honoring her commitments was a priority for Nina. So much so that she disciplined her spending and worked a second job to pay off her debt.

Listening to a person say they believe in Christ and profess to be Christian is quite different from observing behavior and filtering through excuses.

Nina had so many goals and dreams for her life but she spent so many years just drowning and living in a world of bad checks, debt collector phone calls, overdrawn checking accounts, police visits, delinquent taxes, and many, many excuses. This was not who Nina was, yet she was forced to be a part of this lifestyle. Nevertheless, today is a new day and God is still perfecting the work that He has begun. She is encouraged in her walk now more than ever! She watched God carry her through a very difficult season in her life and He has impregnated her with new dreams! She is RESILIENT! She will not give up now! If she has nothing else, she knows that she has HOPE. God has taught her how to trust Him down every path of this maze. He has promised to give her a victorious end and His word will not return void. Hallelujah!